Praise for Edouard Levé

"*Suicide* reads like a photo album. This is no surprise, considering that Levé was as much an accomplished photographer as he was anything else. The prose is clipped, almost terse; while each line can be seen to represent a single idea in just the same way a photo in an album represents one moment in time. [...] *Suicide* is at times beautiful, immensely sad at others, and in more moments than one might want to admit there is the potential in the text to be deeply relatable."
—Tom McCartan, *Three Percent*

"Despite its proliferation of I's, *Autoportrait* paradoxically manages to be as much a book about us, each reader, as Levé. It sucks us into the whirlpool of another mind and spits us back out in our own, where we confront our own flat feet, our habitual failure to fill up ice cube trays, our discomfort in bathrooms next to kitchens."
—Stephen Sparks, *Three Percent*

Books by Edouard Levé
Available in English

Autoportrait
Works
Newspaper

SUICIDE

BY
Edouard Levé

Translated and with
an afterword by
Jan Steyn

DALKEY ARCHIVE PRESS
Dallas, TX / Rochester, NY

Deep Vellum | Dalkey Archive Press
3000 Commerce Street
Dallas, Texas 75226
www.dalkeyarchive.com

Deep Vellum is a 501c3 nonprofit literary arts organization founded in 2013 with the mission to bring the world into conversation through literature.

Text Copyright © 2008 Édouard Levé
Translation copyright © 2011 by Jan Steyn
Afterword copyright © 2011 by Jan Steyn

Originally published in French by Éditions P.O.L, Paris, France, 2008.
First Dalkey Archive Press Edition, 2011
First Dalkey Archive Essentials Edition, 2025
All rights reserved.

Support for this publication has been provided in part by grants from the National Endowment for the Arts, the Texas Commission on the Arts, the City of Dallas Office of Arts and Culture, the Communities Foundation of Texas, and the Addy Foundation.

Library of Congress Cataloging-in-Publication Data
Names: Levé, Édouard, author. | Steyn, Jan H., translator, author of afterword, colophon, etc.
Title: Suicide / by Edouard Levé ; translated and with an afterword by Jan Steyn.
Other titles: Suicide. English Description: Dallas, TX : Dalkey Archive Press, 2025.
Identifiers: LCCN 2025001091 (print) | LCCN 2025001092 (ebook) | ISBN 9781628976106 (trade paperback) | ISBN 9781628976199 (ebook)
Subjects: LCSH: Suicide--Fiction. | LCGFT: Novels. Classification: LCC PQ2712.E87 S8513 2025 (print) | LCC PQ2712.E87 (ebook) | DDC 843/.92--dc23/eng/20250226 LC record available at https://lccn.loc.gov/2025001091 LC ebook record available at https://lccn.loc.gov/2025001092

Cover art and design by Justin Childress
Interior design and typeset by Douglas Suttle
Printed in the United States of America

SUICIDE

One Saturday in the month of August, you leave your home wearing your tennis gear, accompanied by your wife. In the middle of the garden you point out to her that you've forgotten your racket in the house. You go back to look for it, but instead of making your way toward the cupboard in the entryway where you normally keep it, you head down into the basement. Your wife doesn't notice this. She stays outside. The weather is fine. She's making the most of the sun. A few moments later she hears a gunshot. She rushes into the house, cries out your name, notices that the door to the stairway leading to the basement is open, goes down, and finds you there. You've put a bullet in your head with the rifle you had carefully prepared. On the table, you left a comic book open to a double-page spread. In the heat of the moment, your wife leans on the table; the book falls closed before she understands that this was your final message.

    I have never gone into this house. Yet I know the garden, the ground floor, and the basement. I've replayed the scene hundreds of times, always in the same settings, those I imagined upon first hearing the account of your suicide. The house is on a street, it has a roof and a rear façade. Though none of that is real. There's the garden where you go out into the sunlight for the last time and where your wife waits for you. There is the façade she runs toward when she hears the gunshot. There is the entryway where you keep your racket, there's the door to the basement and the stairway. Finally there's the basement where your body lies. It is intact. From what I've been told, your skull hasn't exploded. You're like a young tennis player resting on the lawn after a match. You could be sleeping. You are twenty-five years old. You now know more about death than I do.

Your wife screams. No one is there to hear her, aside from you. The two of you are alone in the house. In tears, she throws herself on you and beats your chest out of love and rage. She takes you in her arms and speaks to you. She sobs and falls against you. Her hands slide over the cold, damp basement floor. Her fingers scrape the ground. She stays for fifteen minutes and feels your body go cold. The telephone brings her out of her torpor. She finds the strength to get up. It's the person with whom you had a tennis date.

"Hello, what's going on? I'm waiting for you."

"He's dead. Dead," she responds.

The scene stops there. Who removed the body? The firemen? The police? Since murder can be disguised as suicide, did a forensic pathologist do an autopsy? Was there an inquest? Who decided that it was a suicide and not a crime? Did they question your wife? Were they sensitive or were they suspicious when talking to her? Did she have the pain of being a suspect added to the pain of your disappearance?

I haven't seen your wife since. I hardly knew her. I met her four or five times. When the two of you got married, you and I stopped seeing each other. I see her face again now. It has remained unchanged for twenty years. I've retained a fixed image of her from the last time I saw her. Memory, like photographs, freezes recollections.

You spent your life in three houses. When your mother was

pregnant with you, your parents lived in a small apartment. Your father didn't want his children to grow up cramped. He used to say "my children," although he only had the one at that point. With your mother, he visited a partially dilapidated château belonging to a retired colonel of the Légion who had never moved in because he deemed the place to be in too great a state of disrepair for it to be habitable. Your father, director of a public works contracting firm, didn't seem put off by the scale of the repairs. Your mother liked the grounds. They moved in, in April. You were born in a clinic on Christmas day. A servant kept three fires going in the château at all times: one in the kitchen, one in the living room, and one in your parents' bedroom, where you slept during the first two years of your life. When your brother was born, repairs had still not progressed. You lived in precarious luxury for three more years, until the birth of your sister. It was after your parents had decided to look for a more comfortable place that your father announced to your mother that he was leaving her. She found a house that was smaller and less beautiful than the château, but warmer and more welcoming. There you had your second bedroom, which you occupied until leaving to live with your wife at twenty-one years of age. The little house you shared with her contained your third bedroom. It was your last.

The first time I saw you, you were in your bedroom. You were seventeen years old. You were living in your mother's house, on the first floor, between your brother's and your sister's bedrooms. You rarely left your room. The door was locked, even when you were inside. Your brother and your sister have no memory of ever entering it. If they had something to tell you, they would speak through the door. No one came in to clean up; you did it yourself. I don't know why you came to open the door for me when I knocked. You didn't ask who it was. What made you guess it was me? My manner of approach, of making the floorboards creak? Your shutters were closed. The room was bathed in a soft red light.

You were listening to "I Talk to the Wind" by King Crimson, and you were smoking. It made me think of a nightclub. It was broad daylight outside.

Your wife only remembered later that before falling from the table, the comic book you had left there was open. Your father bought dozens of copies, which he gave to everyone. He came to know the text and the images of this book by heart; this was not at all like him, but he ended up identifying with the comic. He is looking for the page, and on the page for the sentence, that you had chosen. He keeps a record of his reflections in a file, which is always on his desk and on which is written "Suicide Hypotheses." If you open the cupboard to the left of his desk, you'll find ten identical folders filled with handwritten pages bearing the same label. He cites the captions of the comic book as if they were prophecies.

Since you seldom spoke, you were rarely wrong. You seldom spoke because you seldom went out. If you did go out, you listened and watched. Now, since you no longer speak, you will always be right. In truth, you do still speak: through those, like me, who bring you back to life and interrogate you. We hear your responses and admire their wisdom. If the facts turn out to contradict your counsel, we blame ourselves for having misinterpreted you. Yours are the truths, ours are the errors.

You remain alive insofar as those who have known you outlive you. You will die with the last of them. Unless some of them have made you live on in words, in the memory of their children. For how many generations will you live on like this, as a character from a story?

You went to a concert in Paris. At the end of the first set the singer cut open a vein and sprayed his blood over the first few rows, tracing out circular arcs with his arms. Your brown leather jacket got a few drops on it, which drops then got lost in its general color when they dried. After the concert, you went with the friends who were with you to a café, the name of which you forgot. You spoke to strangers for hours. Afterward you walked the streets in search of other cafés, but they were closed. You stretched out on the park benches of a square near the Gare Saint-Lazare, and you remarked on the shape of the clouds. At six o'clock you had breakfast. At seven you took the first train home. When, the next day, your friends repeated to you the words you had spoken to strangers in the café, you remembered nothing of them. It was as though someone else inside you had spoken. You recognized neither your words, nor your thoughts, but you liked them better than you would have if you had remembered saying them. Often all it took was for someone else to speak your own words back to you for you to like them. You would note down those sayings of yours that were repeated back to you. You were the author of this text twice over.

Your life was a hypothesis. Those who die old are made of the past. Thinking of them, one thinks of what they have done. Thinking of you, one thinks of what you could have become. You were, and you will remain, made up of possibilities.

Your suicide was the most important thing you ever said, but you'll never be able to enjoy the fruits of this labor.

Given that I am speaking to you, are you dead?

If you were still alive, would we be friends? I was more attached to other boys. But time has seen me drift apart from them without my even noticing. All that would be needed to renew the bond would be a telephone call, but none of us are willing to risk the disillusionment of a reunion. Your silence has become a form of eloquence. But they, who can still speak, remain silent. I no longer think of them, those with whom I was formerly so close. But you, who used to be so far-off, distant, mysterious, now seem quite close to me. When I am in doubt, I solicit your advice. Your responses satisfy me better than those the others could give me. You accompany me faithfully wherever I may be. It is they who have disappeared. You are the present.

You are a book that speaks to me whenever I need it. Your death has written your life.

You don't make me sad, but solemn. You impair my incurable frivolity. Whenever I am too spontaneous and self-centered, and, for some reason or other, your face appears to me, I realize again the importance of the people around me. I see things from a perspective I'm rarely able to achieve. I take advantage on your behalf of things you can no longer experience. Dead, you make me more alive.

You were five years old, and you still couldn't manage to slip on a sweater. Although two years your junior, your brother showed you how it's done. Your father belittled you by suggesting, mockingly, that you try to live up to your little brother's example, and in the end declared you incapable of it. Your brother, who admired you just as much as he did your father, was caught between two authorities. Not wanting to hurt anyone, he didn't brag about your father's praise. His modesty completed your humiliation.

You lie alone in a stone tomb upon which your first and last names are engraved in gold lettering. Below can be read the date of your birth and that of your death, separated by twenty-five years.

When I hear of a suicide, I think of you again. Yet, when I hear that someone died of cancer, I don't think of my grandfather and grandmother, who also died of it. They share cancer with millions of others. You, however, own suicide.

A ruin is an accidental aesthetic object. If it becomes beautiful, this was certainly not the intention. A ruin is not constructed or maintained. The tendency of a ruin is to crumble down into a heap. The most beautiful parts remain standing despite their wear and tear. The memory of you is what stays up, your body what subsides. Your ghost remains upright in my memory, while your skeleton is decomposing in the earth.

You were glad to be born on the twenty-fifth of December:

"All the people celebrating don't realize that it's my party too. Being forgotten spares me the trouble of having to shine."

A man once said "I love you" to you. It wasn't me. I didn't feel that way about you while you were alive, but today I can say the same thing, though it wouldn't be the sort of love formerly declared to you. My words come too late. They would not have changed your decision, but they would have changed the way I remember. To love someone from the moment of his death: is that friendship?

I have only one photograph of you. I took it on your birthday. You were at our place. My mother had baked a cake. I had prepared my camera in advance to avoid your having to act out the scene several times for the photo.

I took the photo without a flash while you were blowing out the candles. The image is blurred. It's in black and white. Your cheeks are hollow from blowing, your lips pursed to expel the air. I had composed the shot around you; no one else can be seen. You were wearing a thick woolen sweater. Life rushes from your lungs to put out the flames. You look happy.

Having died young, you will never be old.

Your grandfather used to speak even less than you did. He would smile in silence when passing by with his fishing rod, walking along the line of trees in order to take the path that led along the riverbank that demarcated the boundary of the park and which was where he was going to spend the afternoon. One day, when I was doing stunts on the branches above the water, my watch fell in. Years later, in the run of a dry summer, the river being low, your grandfather found it. I wound it up again. It started. You'd been dead for two years.

A woman who was a friend of yours, whose father-in-law ran a big hotel, got you a summer job. You were a porter and a housekeeper. I had some difficulty imagining you in a bellhop's uniform, with an antique cloak and a red and black cap. Cleaning the rooms, you found some strange objects. One day, in the night-table drawer of a man whom you had identified as "the banker," you discovered a collection of homosexual pornographic magazines, still wrapped in plastic, and a never-used dildo. You showed them to me. You had left the magazines unopened. Were these discovered again after your death? What did people make of their presence in your home?

You often spoke to me about *Ruin of the Garnieri*. Its author, Prospero Miti, didn't use to reread his printed works; he would only look at the proofs. One day, as an exception, he did reread one of them, and he realized that the order of the chapters did not correspond to what he had written. Since he liked the book this way, he didn't ask for future editions to be corrected. You came across this anecdote after having read the book. You never tired of rereading it to try and discover the original order.

You used to take the elevator to go down, but not to go up.

You used to believe that with age you would become less unhappy, because you then would have reasons to be sad. When you were still young, your suffering was inconsolable because you believed it to be unfounded.

Your suicide was scandalously beautiful.

One day, in winter, you set out across the countryside alone on horseback. It was four o'clock. Night fell when you were still kilometers away from the stud farm. A storm was gathering. It broke while you were galloping through desolate fields. The outline of the town was silhouetted in the distance in blue and black. The thunder and lightning did not frighten the beast. You were roused by the onset of tempestuous weather. You clung tight to the creature, its odor amplified by the rain. You finished the trip in soggy darkness, the horse's hooves lashing the loamy earth with each stride.

You preferred reading standing up in bookstores to reading sitting down in libraries. You wanted to discover today's literature, not yesterday's. The past belongs to libraries, the present to bookstores. You were, however, more interested in the dead than in contemporaries. More than anything else, you used to read what you called "the living dead": deceased authors still in print. You trusted publishers to bring yesterday's knowledge into actuality today. You didn't really believe in miraculous discoveries of forgotten authors. You thought time would sort them all out, and that it's better to read authors from the past who are published today than to read today's authors who would be forgotten tomorrow.

There were two bookstores in town. The small one was better than the big one, but the big one allowed you to read without feeling obliged to make a purchase. There were several sales clerks and several rooms; the clients weren't spied on. In the small one, you used to feel the eyes of the owner on you. You didn't go there to discover books, but to buy the ones you had already chosen.

I heard you imitate an old peasant who used to live behind your mother's house, and who condensed his polite greeting—"How are you doing?"—into "Owyiding?" You approached your interlocutor, taking him by the hand as if to greet him normally, but at the last moment you unleashed the peasant's greeting on him. You gave no sign of your intentions. You didn't repeat it for a second round of laughter. You didn't entertain on demand.

You claimed to be smaller in the evening than in the morning because your weight had compressed your vertebrae. You said that the night returned what the day had taken.

You used to smoke American cigarettes. Your bedroom was soaked in their sweet smell. Watching you smoke inspired the desire to do the same. In your hand, a cigarette was a piece of art. Did you like to smoke, or to be seen smoking? You used to blow perfect smoke rings, thick and dense. They would travel for two meters before wrapping themselves around an object and dissolving on it. I remember their trajectory at night against the light of a lamp. The last time I saw you, you had quit smoking, but not drinking. Stroking your belly, you congratulated yourself on having gained weight, though the difference was slight. You had kept your figure.

Explain your suicide? No one risked it.

You couldn't have been said to dance, exactly. Despite the music sounding around you, bodies being carried away by the whirling bass, it didn't get inside you. You used to trace out the steps, but you were mimicking dancing, rather than doing it. You would dance alone. When a look crossed yours, you'd smile like someone caught off guard in an absurd situation.

Your suicide was not preceded by failed attempts.

You did not fear death. You stepped in its path, but without really desiring it: how can one desire something one doesn't know? You didn't deny life but affirmed your taste for the unknown, betting that if something existed on the other side, it would be better than here.

When you read a book, you would return over and again to the page headed "Other Works By . . ." You didn't know if you would want to read the other works, but you delighted in imagining what their titles suggested. You never read Neruda's *Residence on Earth*, for fear that the poems in that collection wouldn't live up to their title. Being unknown, they were more real to you than they would have been if they had disappointed upon reading. During the week you sometimes thought it was Sunday.

You didn't like to travel. You rarely went abroad. You would spend your time in your bedroom. It seemed useless to you to travel for miles in order to stay in a place less comfortable than your own. To think up imaginary holidays was enough for you. You used to jot down in a notebook the things you would have been able to do by following contemporary tourist trends: Watch people at prayer in an Indian temple. Dive in Bali. Ski in Val-d'Isère. Visit an exhibition in Helsinki. Swim in Porto-Vecchio.

When you were sick of your bedroom, you consoled yourself by rereading your notes on these imaginary holidays, and you closed your eyes to visualize them.

One day I asked you why you seldom traveled. You told me the story of that writer, a friend of your mother's, who obtained funding in order to spend a few months abroad. He wanted to do research in order to write a work of political fiction that would take place in an imaginary country, inspired by the real country he went to, which a dictator had brought to its knees thirty years earlier. Having arrived, he understood in a day how absurd his enterprise was: research would be of no use to him. His imagination was everything, but he needed to make the trip in order to understand this obvious fact. His six-month voyage was cut down to two days. He took the first plane home.

I hadn't known you spoke any foreign languages. One day, an Irish friend of your mother's came by. She did not speak French. You addressed her in perfect English.

Only the living seem incoherent. Death closes the series of events that constitutes their lives. So we resign ourselves to finding a meaning for them. To refuse them this would amount to accepting that a life, and thus life itself, is absurd. Yours had not yet attained the coherence of things done. Your death gave it this coherence.

One day, you set off on your blue motorcycle to the coast. You were traveling at 180 kilometers per hour. A car fishtailed into your path. You lifted your arm and signaled your offense as you passed. Thirty kilometers on, when you got off the freeway, the car overtook you and blocked your way at a crossroads. You didn't know what the driver wanted, but he revved his engine as much as he could without moving an inch. There were two men looking at you from the back seat, excited, egging each other on. You got off your motorcycle and headed toward the vehicle. They left before you could get to them. And then, later, at the beach, you ran into them by chance. When they saw you from afar, they believed you had followed them. Again you headed for them, keeping your helmet on. They were in their swimming trunks. They gathered their possessions at top speed and bolted, looking back over their shoulders while running.

In public, your quiet way of observing others made them uncomfortable, as if you were a breathing statue, indifferent to all the frivolous movement that the stillness of a statue so underlines.

Your choosing to erase the world exempts those surviving you from doing so. What you miss, they see. Their pains become pleasures when they think that you are no longer anything at all.

In art, to reduce is to perfect. Your disappearance bestowed a negative beauty on you.

In your mother's house, there were an old watchdog and some passive, useless house cats. We used to repeat the old saw: feed a cat for a lifetime and it will leave you one day; feed a dog for a day and it will be loyal for a lifetime. You were the cat and I the dog.

You succeeded in the few things you undertook.

The last time that I saw you, you were wearing a white cotton shirt. You were standing upright with your wife on the lawn, in the sunlight, in front of the château, at my brother's wedding. You shared in the enthusiasm of the ceremony. For my part, I felt distanced from it. I didn't recognize my family in this mundane get-together. You didn't seem put off by the bourgeois ceremony, or by my brother's choice to have his love approved by third parties, even when these were distant third parties. You didn't have the sad and absent look you normally took on at public gatherings. You smiled, watching the people, a little tipsy from the wine and the sun, chatting on the large lawn between the white stone façade and the two-hundred-year-old cedar tree. I often wondered, after your death, if that smile, the last one I saw from you, was mocking, or if instead it was the kindly smile of someone who knew that soon he would no longer partake in earthly pleasures. You didn't regret leaving these behind, but neither were you averse to enjoying them a little longer.

You did not hesitate. You prepared the shotgun. You put in a shell. You fired into your mouth. You knew that suicide by shotgun could fail when aiming for the temple, the forehead, or the heart, because the recoil throws the gun off its target. With the mouth keeping it steady, errors are rare. If you had wanted to announce your suicide, which is to say renounce it, you would have chosen a gentler method. Yours was violent, the result irreversible. You used to think things through before acting. Once you were decided on something, nothing would stop you. Your gaze was no longer fixed on the world around you, but sighted on your target. Once, your mother's last dog charged at another dog a hundred meters off. It caught up with the other dog, trampled it, took it by its throat, and shook it like a mouse. It would have killed the beast if they hadn't been separated. You had that same look.

Your suicide was an action, but an action with a contrary effect: a form of vitality that produces its own death.

Your wife didn't use to speak when you were present. I don't remember her voice. Her look would indicate her approval or disapproval of you. You were the person she would look at the most, no matter who you were surrounded by. Her shyness would reassure you. Her discretion would accompany your silence. The two of you smoked the same cigarettes. You used to carry a packet for two. She would drive the car and you the motorcycle. You didn't have children. She worked. She earned money for both of you; you studied economics. She admired your theories and your language. What became of her? Has she resigned herself to your death? Does she think of you when she makes love? Did she remarry? In killing yourself, did you also kill her? Did she name a son in your memory? If she has a daughter, does she speak to her of you? What does she do on your birthday? And on the anniversary of your death? Does she put flowers on your grave? Where are the photographs she took of you? Did she keep your clothes? Do they still smell of you? Does she wear your cologne? What did she do with your drawings? Are they framed in a room of her house? Has she erected a museum in your honor? Which men followed after you? Did they know you? Do you, through her memory of you, make the existence of a successor impossible?

When you were awake, stretched out in your bed in the dark, shutters drawn, your thoughts would flow freely. They would grow obscure when you got up and opened the curtains. The violence of daylight would efface the nocturnal clarity. At night, your wife's sleep lent lucidity to your solitude. In the daytime, people were barriers, dividing you up, preventing you from hearing what you listened to at night: the voice of your brain.

You monopolize my memories of sad rock music. When I hear certain songs, they are tainted with your nebulous presence. You didn't use to read poetry, but you would sometimes recite it: the lyrics, without music, of the songs you liked. Rock was your poetry.

You used to say it was better to listen to rock in a foreign language that you knew poorly. How beautiful the words were if they were only half understood. What great stuff Dada would have brought to rock, if only the dates had coincided.

You didn't see a psychoanalyst, but you spent a lot of time analyzing yourself. You read Freud, Jung, and Lacan. You reflected on psychoanalysis, but you didn't practice it. You thought that treatment would normalize you, or banalize the strangeness you cultivated. You used to like listening to others. They trusted you. Quiet, attentive, and constructive, you helped those who placed their confidence in you more than you helped yourself.

You collected phrases spoken on the street by passersby. One of your favorites was: "A canine is just fine, but I do adore a dinosaur."

You collected proper names. You framed an electoral list bringing together candidates with particularly disquieting last names.

You kept a tape of the messages left on your answering machine by mistake. One of them went: "We've arrived fine. We've arrived fine. We've arrived fine." Uttered slowly by an old lady in despair.

We used to talk through the night, only stopping thanks to the dawn. One evening, you spoke for eight hours nonstop, about Freud and Marx, with some interspersed remarks about Kondratiev cycles. Your digressions grew longer in proportion to your consumption of your mother's liquors, mixed at random. Upon daybreak you came up with the "Kondratiev cocktail" by pouring a shot of each of fifteen bottles into one large glass. The Ricard drowned out all other tastes and gave a milky appearance to the beverage. You drank all of it before going to bed.

You kept your day planners from previous years. You reread them when you doubted your existence. You would relive your past by randomly flipping through them as if you were skimming through a chronicle of yourself. You sometimes found appointments you no longer remembered, and people's names, written in your own hand, which meant nothing whatsoever to you. However, you could recall most events. And so you worried about not remembering what happened in between the things you wrote down. You had lived those moments too. Where had they gone?

You refused to be prolific. You would do little, but well, or do nothing rather than do it poorly. You knew nothing of contemporary appetites. You didn't demand to have it all, all at once. You liked to forgo eating, drinking, smoking, speaking, going out. You were able to dispense with light for days on end, happy in your room with the curtains drawn. You didn't miss fresh air. You were thrilled by silence. You made a classicism out of this drought.

You had no taste for spectacle, but choosing death demanded

you choose the place, the time, and the method. In order to achieve this, you were compelled to play the director.

You used to give yourself over to endless sessions of doubt. You would claim to be an expert on the subject. But doubting would tire you so much that you would end up doubting doubt itself. I saw you one day at the end of an afternoon of solitary speculation. You were unmoving and petrified. Running several kilometers in a deep forest full of ravines and pitfalls would have exhausted you less.

Your suicide makes the lives of those who outlive you more intense. Should they be threatened by boredom, or should the absurdity of their lives leap out at them from the curve of some cruel mirror, let them remember you, and the pain of existence will seem preferable to the disquietude of no longer being. What you no longer see, they look at. What you no longer hear, they listen to. The song you no longer sing, they burst into. The joy of simple things appears to them by the light of your sad memory. You are that black but intense glow, which, since the dying of your light, freshly illuminates the day that had become obscure to them.

You went alpine skiing with friends. The first day, you went as high up as you could, to the summit of a glacier that could be seen from the ski station. Your friends came down quickly; they were cold. You stopped, by yourself, in a small valley, to look at the fresh snow that had fallen the previous day. The sun was lighting it up from behind while the wind lifted a slight film from its top layer. In this little valley, the rocks, the shrubs, and the earth were covered by an even, cold whiteness. It was nighttime by day, a negative version of darkness. It seemed to you like sleeping an ideal sleep, awake, lucid, as in your best dreams.

The funeral Mass took place in a small chapel opposite your mother's house. I only went inside it on this one occasion. It was a small gray building next to the road. To go in one had to walk around the back by way of a dirt path. There was no garden, just a tree. I never heard you, while you were alive, pronounce the words "Mass" or "church." But you were on occasion drawn to speak of God, in the sense of an abstract entity, a conversational topic, a curiosity reserved for others. It was strange to hear the priest speak of you, when he didn't even know you. You used to live across the road, but he had only recently been assigned this parish. He gave your eulogy. He said nothing true, nothing false. In his mouth, you could have been anyone. Even though he had prepared his sermon without knowing you, he appeared to be moved while delivering it, as if he was speaking of someone dear to him. I did not doubt his sincerity, though I did believe him to be moved more by death itself than by yours in particular. In mid-Mass, someone started breathing heavily. I didn't see where the panting came from. It sounded like a wild animal trapped in a cul-de-sac after a long chase. Some people rose to their feet to pick your brother up and to lay him out on a row of chairs. His tears had turned into a panic attack. A few minutes later, while he went on sobbing, your sister also began to feel faint. She too was stretched out. Two creatures distraught by the sadness of your burial. Your mother was still upright, however. The priest, perturbed, pursued his sermon. At the exit, people didn't dare look at each other, it was as if they felt guilty. Of what? Your mother, her head lowered, came forward slowly, supporting herself on the arm of your stepfather. Your father, standing back, felt most guilty. But his guilt was your final humiliation: he appropriated your death for himself by holding himself responsible.

 Your taste for literature did not come from your father, who read little, but from your mother, who taught it. You wondered how, being so different, they could have formed a union; but you noted that in you there was a mixture of the violence of the one and the gentleness of the other. Your father exerted his violence on others. Your mother was sympathetic to the suffering of others. One day you directed the violence you had inherited toward yourself. You dished it out like your father and you took it like your mother.

You liked old things, but not the ones that could be found in flea markets. To know that an object had belonged to others bothered you less than to be ignorant of the identity of its previous owner.

The surface of your body displayed no fat to bear witness to former gustatory excesses. You were thin, muscled, sinewy. Your face used to seem tense, but I understood one afternoon seeing you asleep on a chaise longue, nerves at rest, that the impression originated from the sharp and angular morphology of your features.

You used to speak without gesturing. When you were silent, rather than your body, it was your eyes that were expressive. Your face was so rarely animated that you could incite laughter or intimidate someone simply by pursing your lips.

Your life was less sad than your suicide might suggest. You were said to have died of suffering. But there was not as much sadness in you as there is now in those who remember you. You died because you searched for happiness at the risk of finding the void. We shall have to wait for death before we can know what it is that you found. Or before leaving off knowing anything at all, if it is to be silence and emptiness that awaits us.

The way in which you quit it rewrote the story of your life in a negative form. Those who knew you reread each of your acts in the light of your last. Henceforth, the shadow of this tall black tree hides the forest that was your life. When you are spoken of, it begins with recounting your death, before going back to explain it. Isn't it peculiar how this final gesture inverts your biography? I've never heard a single person, since your death, tell your life's story starting at the beginning. Your suicide has become the foundational act, and those earlier acts that you had hoped to relieve of their burden of meaning by way of this gesture, the absurdity of which so attracted you, have ended up simply alienated instead. Your final second changed your life in the eyes of others. You are like the actor who, at the end of the play, with a final word, reveals that he is a different character than the one he appeared to be playing.

You are not among those who ended up sick and old, with withered ghostly bodies, resembling death before they've stopped living. Their demise is the fulfillment of their decrepitude. A ruin that dies: is this not deliverance, is it not the death of death? As for you, you departed in vitality. Young, lively, healthy. Your death was the death of life. Yet I like to think that you embodied the opposite: the life of death. I don't try to explain to myself in what form you might have survived your suicide, but your disappearance is so unacceptable that the following lunacy was born along with it: a belief in your eternity.

You didn't go to Peru; you didn't like black boots; you never walked barefoot on a rosy, pebbled path. The sheer number of things you didn't do is dizzying, because it throws light on the number of things we will ourselves be stripped of. For us, there will never be enough time. You chose to eschew more time. You renounced the future, the future that allows for survival, because we believe it is infinite. We want to be able to embrace all the earth, to taste all its fruits, to love all men. You rejected these illusions, which feed us with hope.

While traveling, a new destination would seem more desirable to you than wherever you were, right up to the moment you got there and found that your dissatisfaction had followed you: the mirage had shifted to the next stopover point. Yet your preceding stops would become more attractive as you got further away from them. For you, the past would be forever improving, the future would draw you forward, but the present would weigh you down.

When you traveled, it was to taste the pleasures of being a stranger in a strange town. You were a spectator and not an actor:

mobile voyeur, silent listener, accidental tourist. At random, you would visit public spaces, squares, streets, and parks. You would go into stores, restaurants, churches, and museums. You liked public places where no one was surprised if you stood still in the middle of the urban flux. The crowd guaranteed your anonymity. Property seemed to be abolished. Yet those buildings, those sidewalks, and those walls did belong to someone, though nothing forced you to acknowledge this fact. The opacity of local languages and customs would prevent you from knowing, or guessing, to whom it was that they belonged. You used to drift through a visual form of communism, according to which things belonged to those who looked at them. In the midst of this utopia, which only your fellow lone voyagers would perceive, you used to transgress society's rules unknowingly, and no one would hold you accountable for it. You would mistakenly enter private residences, go to concerts to which you had not been invited, eat at community banquets where you could only guess the community's identity when they started giving speeches. Had you behaved like this in your own country, you would have been taken for a liar or a fool. But the improbable ways of a foreigner are accepted. Far from your home, you used to taste the pleasure of being mad without being alienated, of being an imbecile without renouncing your intelligence, of being an impostor without culpability.

You wanted to treat foreign lands as though they were friends with whom you could have a tête-à-tête in a café, as equals. When you traveled with company, the country would shrink away; your companion would become the subject of your voyage as much as the country itself. As for group travel, the country would end up being the silent host whose presence one forgets like one does an overly timid guest, the principal subject becoming the backdrop. At the end of an amusing trip to England with a very talkative group, you decided that that was the end of adult vacation camps for you. You had gone in the company of the blind. Henceforth you would travel in order to see. And you would travel alone, so as to dissolve into the spectacle of the unknown. The facts belied these decisions: you no longer traveled abroad.

Sitting in a café, a few seconds looking at passersby would be enough for you to label them with a few incisive words. You would create an entire cruel category out of a person or detail. Fifty-year-old virgin, very tall dwarf, ogre in a smock, right-wing swinger, salesman with a flashy bracelet, little man in heels, pedophile accountant, hetero fag: your company would be struck by the appropriateness of these labels, eliciting from them a hilarity far more malevolent than your own. You were neither malicious nor cynical, just pitiless. After a session of panoramic crowd-gazing through the windows of a brasserie in the city center on a Saturday afternoon, after leaving you, one wondered how you would have described your own friends if they had passed in front of you a few seconds earlier. And shivered at the idea that your piercing eye might detect in each of them the incarnation of a type.

You used to read dictionaries like other people read novels. Each entry is a character, you'd say, who might be encountered on some other page. Plots, many of them, would form during any random reading. The story changes according to the order in which the entries are read. A dictionary resembles the world more than a novel does, because the world is not a coherent sequence of actions but a constellation of things perceived. It is looked at, unrelated things congregate, and geographic proximity gives them meaning. If events follow each other, they are believed to be a story. But in a dictionary, time doesn't exist: ABC is neither more nor less chronological than BCA. To portray your life in order would be absurd: I remember you at random. My brain resurrects you through stochastic details, like picking marbles out of a bag.

Not one to believe stories, you would pay them only a floating sort of attention, looking for the hitch. Your body was there, but your mind would depart, then reappear, like an auditory form of blinking. You would reconstitute accounts in an order different from that which they'd been given. You would perceive duration like others would look at an object in three dimensions, moving yourself around it so as to be able to represent it in all its aspects at once. You looked for the most immediate impression of other people, the photograph that would, in a second, capture the unfolding of their years. You reconstituted their lives through a panoramic lens. You brought together distant events by compressing time so that each instant stood side by side with the others. You translated duration into space. You looked for the aleph of the other.

The private tennis court of a neighboring residence had been abandoned. Even in its heyday, it was only put to use for ten days of the year. Poorly maintained, it ended up being forgotten, the net sagging in the middle, the white lines darkened, the clay invaded by green mushrooms. You used to see it through the thuja trees, at the edge of the property's grounds, surrounded by a rusty fence, abandoned by adults, rediscovered on certain Sundays by children, similar to a haunted house where ghosts in old-fashioned sports outfits would prowl about in broad daylight. It frightened you in the same way as it did to see a twenty-year-old vagrant or a beautiful lame girl: broken figures, half alive. Though you saw your own self-portrait in it, you did not avoid this modern ruin. Passing in front of it was like coming into contact with a memento mori. Metaphors of death troubled you, but you did not decline their spectacle. They were trials to be overcome in order to appreciate life, by remembering its opposite.

You were not surprised to feel yourself ill adapted to the world, but it did surprise you that the world had produced a being who now lived in it as a foreigner. Do plants commit suicide? Do animals die of hopelessness? They either function or disappear. You were perhaps a weak link, an accidental evolutionary dead end, a temporary anomaly not destined to burgeon again.

You used to forget details. You would have made a poor witness, if asked to reconstruct the order of events preceding an accident. But your slowness and your immobility allowed you to observe the collective action in slow motion, and to see things that, because of their urgency and the profusion of detail, would escape the notice of others. In a small provincial town, looking at a market from a hotel room above it, you grasped that the crowd moving below traced out a triangle that would swell and shrink in cycles. A futile observation? A useless sort of science? Your intelligence did not disdain gratuitous subjects.

Facing your mirror, happy or carefree, you were someone. Unhappy, you weren't anyone any longer: the lines of your face would fade; you would recognize what you habitually used to call "me," but you would see someone else looking at you. Your gaze would sweep across your face as if it were made of air: the eyes opposite you would be unfathomable. To animate your features with a wink or a grimace would be of no help: deprived of reason, the expression would be artificial. And so you would play at miming conversations with imaginary third parties. You would believe yourself to be going mad, but the ridiculousness of your situation would end up making you laugh. Acting out the roles in a comedy sketch would let you exist anew. You would become yourself again by embodying someone else. Your eyes would now rest on themselves and, facing the mirror, you could again say your name without it sounding like an abstraction.

You used to believe in written things regardless of whether they were true or false. If they were lies, their traces would one day serve as evidence that could be turned against their authors: the truth had merely been deferred. Moreover, liars write less than they speak. In books, life, whether it was documented or invented, seemed to you more real than the life you saw and heard for yourself. It was when you were alone that you used to perceive real life. When you recalled it, it was made weaker by your memory's many points of imprecision. But others had imagined life in books: what you were reading was the superimposition of two consciousnesses, yours and that of the author. You used to doubt what you had perceived, but never what others invented. You suffered real life in its continuous stream, but you controlled the flow of fictional life by reading at your own rhythm: you could stop, speed up, or slow down; go backward or jump into the future. As a reader, you had the power of a god: time submitted to you. As for words, even the best-chosen ones, they passed like the wind. They would leave traces in your memory, but your recollecting them made you doubt their existence. Did you reconstruct them as they had been spoken, or did you remodel them in your own style?

One evening you were invited to dine at a friend's house with other guests. To the host who, opening the door for you on your arrival, asked you how you were doing, you responded, "Badly." Disconcerted, the host didn't know what to say—all the more so because you were standing in his doorway, and because when you had rung the bell, an enthusiastic and impatient "Ahhh!" from the assembly of guests gathered in the living room had resounded through the walls. The two of you couldn't simply engage there and then in a brief conversation about your suffering, but neither could you make the others wait without having to give explanations to them, all the more embarrassing since your explanations would be addressed to a group of friends gathered to have a good time. You didn't want to disrupt the party, but you couldn't make yourself lie in response to the simple question, "How are you doing?" You were more honest than courteous. Even though you were capable of it, it seemed unthinkable to you to put on a show of well-being for a close friend. Having arrived in the living room, you did not want to reproduce the unease sparked by your first response. To your friend's friends, some of whom you didn't know, you presented a friendly exterior. In this atmosphere, which made you feel foreign, you were surprised at your success in putting on the appropriate face, which, if it didn't contribute to the general euphoria, at least didn't destroy the mood with its indifference.

Your pain died down with nightfall. The possibility of happiness began at five o'clock in the winter, later in the summer.

You were surprised that your state of mind could be so variable without those around you noticing. Once you confessed to someone that you had been very depressed when dining with her several months earlier. She was stunned, discovering her blindness like a time bomb. And you, faithful, kept a straight face.

You were such a perfectionist that you wanted to perfect perfecting. But how can one judge whether perfection has been attained? Why not go on and modify yet another detail? There always came, however, that terrifying moment when you could no longer judge the improvements you'd brought about: your taste for perfect things bordered on madness. You would lose your frame of reference; you would work in a blank, in the midst of vague and clouded visions. What was difficult for you wasn't beginning or continuing, but finishing; that is to say, deciding, one day, that your project could no longer be reworked without suffering from it—that an addition would diminish it rather than improve it. Sometimes, weary of perfecting perfections, you would abandon your work without destroying it or finishing it. To look at these abandoned imperfections should have reassured you: you had at least worked, even if your attic only contained works that had been abandoned. But the sight of them caused you anguish: being pragmatic, you wanted to see what you had produced function. Your taste for abbreviation meant that instead of finishing the works you undertook, you finished yourself.

You were a virtuoso on the drums. As a teenager, you were in three rock bands: Les Atomes, Crise 17, and Dragonfly. You also sang, and you wrote the lyrics to some songs that you would play in front of a few friends, at parties or in basements on loan from parents. Your bands split up in so far as the members left the high school or the town to go live elsewhere with their parents. You stayed put, and you stopped playing in bands. You continued to practice in your basement, accompanying recorded music played through a powerful amplifier, or playing solos that could last for hours. You would come out exhausted, but exalted, as after a long trance. Some years later, when you were twenty-two, Damien, the guitarist from Dragonfly, got back in touch with you to replace the absent drummer for a concert that his current band, Lucide Lucinda, was giving in Bordeaux. When buying your train ticket, you decided to stay in Bordeaux for three days to see the town, which you did not know. The concert took place on the night of your arrival, in a center for contemporary art, on the occasion of the opening of an exhibition with the participation of the guitarist who had in the meantime become an artist. There was a crowd of young art- and music-lovers. During rehearsal, you discovered that you had lost nothing of your gift for playing in a band. Lucide Lucinda's music was simple and effective, like English rock from the 1960s, to which the group paid tribute. After the concert you surveyed the exhibition accompanied by the musicians and their friends. You spent part of the evening with a young, tall, thin, blonde Polish artist who was exhibiting giant sculptures in the shape of organs or stones, made out of fragments of plastic mineral-water bottles. You were surprised that her hands, which were so thin, had executed such monumental work. The tops of her hands were intact, but when she reached out to show you a detail on one of the sculptures, you discovered scars on the inside of her palm and on two of her fingers. Her patient and slow assembly work succeeded, through the accumulation of small fragments, in producing vast objects. You made the analogy with your solitary musical sessions: you used to spend hours producing sounds that would vanish in the solitude of your basement, where you were your only audience. She edified, you dispersed yourself. The night was spent in various bars in the middle of town and in a nightclub with high-tech Japanese décor where you watched people dance while you drank cocktails. The next day you woke up in the room reserved for you in a two-star hotel. The wallpaper was yellow and the carpet royal blue, ornamented with the motif of the logo of this particular chain of cheap hotels. The window looked out onto a narrow white courtyard, in which the sun cast a violent light. The silence of this anonymous place plunged you into a hazy anguish. You knew nothing about this town that you had barely researched. You were going to explore it at random, asking around for information from strangers about places to visit. Shaving, you believed you saw a stranger in the mirror. It was indeed your face, but the décor, which was alien to you, and the absurdity of the situation, made you think that you were someone else. Your self-pity would have made you cry had the telephone not rung. Who could be calling you? You picked up the receiver; it was your wife, who wanted to hear your news. Her voice, which ought to have reassured you, did nothing but reinforce, at a distance, your feeling of solitude. You told her that the concert had gone well, and you pretended to be enthusiastic about the idea of the two days of discovery afforded you. After hanging up, while you were preparing to leave the hotel, the telephone began to ring again. It was Damien, proposing you go with him to a techno music festival on a beach at Biscarrosse. You were tempted to follow him there in order to make the most of his company and that of the musicians. But you had decided to go see the town, and the idea of hanging out with hundreds of strangers in an atmosphere of deafening music was off-putting to you. Despite his disappointment, Damien suggested some places to go see in town. Putting down the phone you would have regretted your decision had you not known that wavering made you suffer more than deciding did. You went out into the street, map in hand. You were in the center of the old town. You took a big pedestrian road, which stretched out for hundreds of meters. You looked into the fashion boutiques, the pâtisseries, the succession of shops of all kinds. There were no surprises waiting for you in this commercial hub. You arrived at a small square dominated by the post office. Disoriented old people had beached themselves on benches. A fifty-something man, to whose belt were attached several plastic shopping bags containing all his personal effects, walked by lifting one shoulder, then the next, in rhythm with his steps. He pointed with his index finger at invisible objects and murmured incomprehensible words. Other than you, no one paid him any attention. You guessed from this that he lived in the neighborhood, and that this square was his living room. Other homeless people hung around, some sitting on the ground, others standing still, waiting for who knows what. They were indifferent to each other; the passersby didn't know they were there. They had become invisible. You approached a street sign in order to know where you were. The plaque indicated, as if in ironic commentary, "Place Saint-Projet." You headed in the direction of the Saint-André Cathedral. The size of this gothic building impressed you; you went inside, but the darkness and the cold immediately put you off. Aside from some foreign tourists following a guide, the church was solely occupied by old ladies who were praying, seated or kneeling. The paintings referred to by a laminated sign at the entrance were hardly visible, so bad was the failing light. You went back out and, after having walked alongside the city hall, walked in the direction of the Musée des Beaux-Arts. Workers were restoring the building and sanding the large stones of the façade. You made your way through the flood of dust that the wind was blowing onto the main door and the bordering lawn. Inside, the two caretakers and the cashier were the only human presence. You perused the halls, where there was a succession of old paintings of the Italian, French, English, Flemish, and German schools. You looked at them distractedly, despite the quality of some of the works. You had the impression of having already seen this museum dozens of times, in other cities. Religious and mythological painting would take you back to a past that was known and without surprises. In provincial museums, you used to look for the most unusual paintings of little-known local masters, the originality of which derived from their minor subjects or clumsy workmanship. This kind of originality was in short supply here, unless it was in the form of a monumental panorama of the Garonne quays. The image showed commercial and maritime activity stretched out for kilometers, with innumerable details. Dozens of characters, small relative to the represented space, brought scenes to life representing the entire social spectrum. The town, idealized by a warm glow, appeared to you in an entirely different light. Perhaps you needed the mediation of an image to appreciate the urban landscape. You stayed for an hour in order to itemize the scenes in the image, to scrutinize its works of architecture, to submerge yourself in this film painted two hundred years ago, a film whose scenario you could, in your own way, have recomposed today. A few footsteps behind you brought you out of your reverie. A bored caretaker was watching you from a distance. You finished your visit in a minute: your immersion in the panorama had prevented you from paying attention to the eighteenth-century portraits around you, despite their merit. You didn't even linger in front of the one of John Hunter by Thomas Lawrence. Your footsteps echoed in the vast gallery through which no other visitor paced. You left the museum under a cloud of white dust and started down the straight, bourgeois, elegant streets of a residential neighborhood. You looked around, furtively discovering interiors you would not see again. Along the sidewalk, the terraces of restaurants received office workers in suits, tourists, retirees. You were hungry, but you didn't want to eat alone in a restaurant. You preferred to buy a sandwich at a bakery and to eat it on a corner in front of a public square, watching the procession of passersby. A girl came up to you to ask for a cigarette. You gave her two; she looked at you, surprised, and exaggeratedly thanked you. On your map you looked for the coordinates of a photography gallery that Damien had suggested to you. It was situated on the other side of town. Judging by the distance, it would have taken you more than an hour to get there. You passed back through the old town, relaxed. Having a goal to your walk was soothing to you. You walked along the Garonne; the quay was closed for construction; they were building a tramway. The construction works disfigured the road and pavement; you had to skirt around fences, cross over piles of sand and avoid holes dug out of the sidewalk. The fronts of old dilapidated warehouses were being renovated one by one as the construction advanced. You paid more attention to the part of town undergoing mutation than to those parts fixed in old and beautiful neighborhoods. There you imagined the life to come: the cityscape existed less for what it was than for what would soon be. Between the town as it was at present, which you had crossed, or the town of the future that your mind constructed based on what your eyes gave it to see, you preferred the town of the past, which the panorama in the museum had shown to you. The photography gallery was located near the port, amid industrial warehouses surrounded by shipping containers and other materials. You walked alongside several sheds and ended up entering into a large gray and white space lit by bay windows situated high up. The exhibition, "New Urban Zones," presented the work of ten photographers who had surveyed the territories of Europe. Few clues permitted one to say where these views had been captured. The landscape portraits showed anonymous places, industrial or commercial zones in the suburbs of modern towns, often on the borderlines between urban and rural areas. There were no people to be seen. The only human presence hinted at was in the cars on the roads. The color prints in large format were lined up as anonymously as the places they represented. It was difficult to distinguish one photograph from another. The framing was frontal, the colors flat, the prints carefully executed. You couldn't succeed in desiring these non-places offered to your view. The photographers had wanted neither to magnify nor to dramatize their subjects. The neutrality of their style recalled those of the buildings they had photographed. Life seemed to have escaped them. You thought the photographers were correct: who could have wanted to live in those thankless, immense, and deserted places? Leaving the gallery again, you found that the port zone could easily have figured among them. But the wind, the bustle of life, the movement of people and vehicles that animated it made the zone habitable. Was this a case of photography killing life by freezing it? It was six in the evening. Museums, galleries, and monuments were closing. You found yourself alone in the town without anything else to do but walk the streets and look at shops, restaurants, architecture. You took the same road back you had come by in order to look at the urban landscape from an inverse point of view. You counted the buildings that you did not remember seeing earlier. There were dozens. You no longer believed in the hypothesis that everything is recorded in memory, but that we are only capable of recalling some of it, according to memory's caprices. Between the next two roads, nine buildings appeared. Only three of them were familiar to you. Each possessed one remarkable detail. The front door of one was adorned with a lion's head painted in blue. A totalizator, for gambling on horse racing, was installed on the ground floor of another, and the windows of the last, recently restored, were still covered in a green plastic film. Only two of the other buildings had distinctive marks. On one a golden plaque stated: "Charles Dreyfus, Psychoanalyst," and the other contained a store selling scuba gear, in the display window of which two divers dressed in yellow and black, equipped with masks and fins, were floating in the middle of a subaquatic universe consisting of regulator valves, spear guns, electric torches, watches, snorkels, buoys, knives, and weights. You asked yourself how, on the one hand, the inscription, which announced to passersby a room where confidences are shared, or, on the other, this gleaming and comical window, could have escaped your attention. Had you been looking at the other side of the street, in the direction of the Garonne? Had you been lost in thought or in the emptiness of the walk? You looked for explanations rather than believe in the shortcomings of your memory. Following your itinerary in reverse however confirmed to you that there now remained only scraps of what you had seen earlier, heading in the other direction. You continued on surrounded by scenery, the majority of whose details were unknown to you. Having come close to the big theater, you considered turning back again in order to verify whether, on a third passing, your memory would be more reliable. But you were hungry. You entered a restaurant decorated with antique woodwork and old tables with marble tops. Some elderly regulars were drinking aperitifs while waiters were spreading tablecloths for the meal. "Will you be dining with us?" a waiter asked at the moment you told yourself that the place was too sad to spend an evening in alone. You told him that you were looking for someone, and after scanning the room you left. You wandered about for an hour looking for a modern restaurant. Night had fallen when you discovered, in a pedestrian cul-de-sac, a chic wine bar, softly lit, where they served tapas. The place was welcoming. Thirty-odd young people were chatting at the bar while slow electronic music created a relaxed atmosphere. Some low tables were occupied by groups of friends. You took up a place in a corner, on the windowed terrace in order to be able to observe the patrons at the bar at the same time as people on the street. But the cul-de-sac was empty, and the only people circulating there were those coming to the bar or leaving it. You ordered squid, ham, chili peppers, chorizo sausage, and cured pork loin with half a bottle of rioja. You had already eaten half your meal when the Polish artist with whom you had passed the previous evening came in looking for some friends. She did not see you and headed in their direction. You hesitated to interrupt her; you did not want to meet new people you would not see again after leaving the city. But not to show yourself, when you were alone, seemed to you absurd, especially since you could not keep from looking at her. She turned toward you, recognized you, and gave you a big smile. You in turn smiled at her, embarrassed to think that she might believe you had wanted to shrug her off: given your position, you could not help but have seen her. You both hesitated to make the first move toward the other. You looked at each other for what seemed to you an endless amount of time. You got up at last and made to join her. The introductions done with, you suggested she join you at your table, without including her friends. She accepted, despite the impoliteness of your proposal. You asked her questions about her life in Poland, about her family and her art. She replied at length and with precision, but when she in turn asked questions of you, you responded with more questions. You had no desire to talk about yourself, but you could have listened to her talk about herself for hours. You wondered if you were trying to seduce her, and whether this had occurred to her. What would you do if her friends left without her and if she walked you to the door of your hotel? You were faithful to your wife, but wasn't that because, in the town where you lived, there was no opportunity to cheat on her? You remembered the opportunities that you had been given for liaisons with women who crossed your path far from your home. You had never yielded. This evening, when this woman suggested going for a drink elsewhere, and when you understood that her friends had discreetly left, you decided to go back to your hotel. She went with you. Having arrived at the threshold, neither of you spoke. You remained standing there without speaking, looking at one another. The moment she slowly approached, you told her that you were going to bed. She smiled at you, and you left her after having gotten her contact information. In your room, you regretted nothing, and you fell asleep, in spite of feeling as though you passed the day simply killing the time that separated you from your return. The next day, you were awakened by this same impression of vacuity. You made the same gestures as the day before, getting up, opening curtains, shaving, and washing. You went down for breakfast in the dining room. It was empty; it was nearly ten o'clock. You read a local newspaper from the day before, cursorily. Back upstairs in your room, you hardly remembered the news you had just learned. You went back out, and set off at random into the town. But your steps spontaneously led you to the same locations that you had strolled through the day before. You paid less attention to what you were looking at; the places no longer had the attraction of novelty. You then decided to walk taking the first street on the right, the second street on the left, the first street on the right and so on, without deviating from this method, so as to not let yourself be guided by the appeal of whatever turned up. You passed the day in this way, looking on your map from time to time at where chance was leading you. You had lunch in a café on a square, in a working-class neighborhood nearly five kilometers from the city center. You watched the passersby and you gathered statistics to keep yourself busy. You counted the number of women, men, and children. You classified people by age, by their probable jobs, or according to more subjective criteria, like the taste revealed by their clothing, or the strangeness of their gait. You stayed for two hours doing this on the terrace of the café. After having reread these statistics, you were struck by their absurdity. What meaning did this inventory have, for which no one had any use and with which you would do nothing? You tore up the pages and you threw them in the gutter. It was three o'clock. Rather than resuming your random walk, you returned by the shortest route to the city center. When you got close to your hotel, it was still too early for dinner. You decided to take the same route as the day before, to verify if what you had seen was now anchored in your memory. You didn't look at the map, you didn't hesitate once over changes in direction. You noticed the same details, signs, sidewalks, roadwork. Only the passersby broke the monotony of the spectacle. You felt your body tiring; this urban strolling was turning into an accidental gymnastic exercise. Having come back to your point of departure, you had lost any notion of time. You looked at your watch and were flabbergasted to discover that four hours had slipped by. You decided to dine in the first restaurant that offered itself to you. It was the Clos Saint-Vivien, a restaurant with traditional bourgeois cooking, elegantly decorated. You chose the first dishes from each section of the menu, a foie gras with mango preserves, a rib steak with bordelaise sauce and sautéed potatoes, and a raspberry cake. The hushed atmosphere reassured you, but the marked attention of the waiters watching you in order to respond to your wishes weighed on you increasingly as the other customers left the restaurant. Before the last couple could leave, you paid the bill and left the restaurant. It was twelve thirty. Back at your hotel, you took notes on the last two days. You described what you had seen, done, and thought. While you believed that you had only passed through a zone of emptiness, the writing of this text kept you up until five in the morning. When you reread it the next day on the train that was carrying you back home, you added numerous notes in the margin. And when your wife asked you what you had done, you spent the entire night telling her, with innumerable details. You had felt idle in this city through which you had paced only to kill time. But the emptiness that you believed yourself to be confronted with was an illusion: you had filled those moments with sensations all the more powerful in that nothing and no one had distracted you from them.

You directed toward yourself a violence that you did not feel toward others. For them you reserved all your patience and tolerance.

You used to tick the wrong boxes on administrative forms to fabricate a new identity for yourself under your own name. Sometimes you would tick "Yes" for "I am on maternity leave," write "3" for "Number of children," and write "Australian" for "Nationality."

You thought that beautiful music was sad, and that sad architecture was ugly.

You didn't vary the registers of friendship. You were predictable and reassuring, like a large stone on the edge of a path. You recounted, with a hint of a smile, the flip-flopping of that cousin of yours who complained to an old friend of recurring back pain and then, fifteen minutes later at the same cocktail party, exclaimed to another that he hadn't felt so good in years. What logic underlay such behavior? Loss of self? Unconscious contradiction? Calculated lie?

The phrase "A long, black song" resurfaced in your consciousness unexpectedly. Where had you heard it? No memory came back to you: the effacement of its origins accentuated its ghostly character.

You marveled at the story of the Parisian entrepreneur whose obsessive hobby consisted in documenting his daily existence. He saved letters, invitation cards, train tickets, bus tickets, metro tickets, tickets for trips by planes or by boat, his contracts, hotel stationary, restaurant menus, tourist guides from countries visited, programs from plays, day planners, notebooks, photographs . . . A room in his house, lined with file cabinets, served as the receptacle for his archives, always being expanded. At the center, organized in a spiral, a chronologically oriented plan indicated Paris, France, or abroad, continents, seas, months, days in different colors. With a glance, the man could visualize his entire existence. He had made a collection of himself.

In front of an object whose function you did not know, but which you knew you could understand if you made the effort, you sometimes preferred to remain at the stage of speculation and spectacle, as when you basked in front of a beautiful landscape: to see it from a distance was enough for you; you didn't need to walk through it. To catch sight of an island from a boat could be more pleasurable than ever setting foot on it.

You undertook the project of designing your own tomb. You didn't want to leave the delicate choice of your most enduring residence to others. It would be made from shiny, flat, and unadorned black marble. In front of it, a stele would indicate your name, your birth date, but also that of your death, at eighty-five years old. It would not be a family tomb: you would occupy it alone. The dates would be engraved during your lifetime.

You imagined the reactions of those walking through the cemetery, seeing a date of death in anticipation, located several decades in the future. Many scenarios could follow.

Before your death, its date, set in advance, would turn your grave into a joke, or else a troubling prediction. If you died before the planned date, you could be buried, and the indicated date could be replaced with that of your actual death—which, in giving the lie to the original inscription, would trivialize your grave. But, you could also be buried without changing the inscription. Visitors, believing it to be a joke, would laugh in front of a tomb which nonetheless would contain a corpse. The stele would carry this joke up to what would be your eighty-fifth year. After this date, those who walked by would no longer have any idea of your eccentricity: who would imagine that the inscription was false, and that the man in the tomb had not died on the date indicated?

Or you would die in the forecasted year, at the age of eighty-five. Either naturally, which would be extraordinary, since your death would be fulfilling your prediction, or by your committing suicide, if you intended to keep the promise carved in marble. You could then be buried without the inscription on the stele being altered in the least.

If you lived past eighty-five, passersby reading the dates would believe you to be dead, even though you would still be alive. And the day would come when you did die. If the stele was left unaltered, you would be buried in a grave whose inscription made you younger. Unless you decided in the end that the inscription should indeed be updated to match the date of your death. Or you left posthumous instructions for someone to perpetually push the inscribed date of your death further back, so that it would always be forecasted, but never achieved.

Your suicide put an end to these complex hypotheses, but your wife, who knew of your project, had your tomb built according to the drawings that you left. She had the dates of your real birth and your death engraved on the black stele. Twenty-five years separate them, not eighty-five: it didn't occur to anyone but you to joke about your death.

It was as easy for you to meet new people face-to-face as it was difficult to meet them in a group. One day, I had invited you to come to breakfast at my parents' family home, a few kilometers from where you lived. We should have been alone, but toward the end of the morning, several friends surprised me by paying me a visit and I suggested that they stay for the meal. When you appeared at the corner of the house, as we were having an aperitif in the sun, you discovered a table set for six instead of two. Your expression fell apart in a second. It recomposed itself when you saw that I had understood that you were upset. You didn't try to hide your feelings from me, but wanted to avoid the impoliteness of seeming disagreeable to my friends. I knew that you would have preferred to turn on your heels and go home right away rather than stay and converse with people you would never see again. They all knew each other well. You had a gift for perceiving in an instant how long- or short-lived friendships were, from the amount of noise a conversation generated, from the liveliness of the voices, from the play of glances. You would have preferred to join a group of strangers getting to know each other rather than this tribe that had formed so far from you, so long ago. But you made the effort to stay. You spoke all afternoon to the same woman, who you succeeded in keeping at arm's length, near the chestnut tree, then under the cedar. Your attraction was reciprocated, but you couldn't manage to disassociate her from the group in which you had discovered her. The shadow of the others hung over her. Looking at her, you worried you wouldn't be able to forget the imprint of her friends. You refused to be the odd one out. Even if this group welcomed you, you would remain the latecomer. To the already-constituted friendships that one joins as a stranger, you preferred those that came together in your presence; the latter you saw being born and developing, and though you couldn't predict which particular affections would weave themselves together, you knew it would all happen at the same time, you would all be equal facing the future. By the end of this day, you understood that the common past of my friends would always keep you at a distance. You preferred not approaching the circle to having to remain at its edge.

You successfully passed the written examination allowing you entrance into a *grande école*. In the oral part of the admissions examination, for the general culture test, you had half an hour to prepare a speech on the topic: "Must one be afraid of having to live one's death?" You felt dizzy before this paradoxical formulation. Can death be lived? Yes, the question implied, since it asked whether such should be feared. You were twenty years old. Up until then, you had thought of death as a phenomenon that occurred only to others and which, when it happened to you, would carry you off without your being conscious of it. To live death—was this to see it coming and to welcome it, rather than abruptly undergoing it, without having the time to feel oneself departing? Was this to choose it by anticipation in order to affirm one's free will before the ineluctable? These questions rattled in your mind, and, on your blank page, you took disordered notes. Among them this one, which you cited to me later: "Death is a country of which nothing is known; no one has returned to describe it." The question was too important to you for you to be able to take some distance from it. The half hour flowed by without you succeeding in putting your ideas in order. You entered a hall where two examiners, seated behind a table, greeted you coldly. You took your place and began to enunciate the ideas you had noted down in the chaotic order they appeared. You believed you read disappointment in your examiners' faces. They remained silent while the words left your mouth mechanically, as if pronounced by someone else. You repeated aloud the meanderings of your thought. One of the two men took up one of your affirmations in a questioning tone: "Death is to life what birth is to the absence of life?" A long silence followed. You didn't respond, petrified, as if death were addressing you in person. It wasn't embodied in the examiners; it prowled about the room between them and you. You were now just waiting for the test to end: passing this exam was no longer important. Though when leaving the room you were certain of having failed it, you were not sorry to have taken the test. To have perceived death, and the incomprehension accompanying it, was more important to you than the results. Later, you were told that you had been accepted. Your speech about death had received one of the highest grades. You refused to enter the school.

    You would have liked to receive, along with invitations, the menus of the dinners to which you had been invited, in order to delight in advance over the dishes you would consume. To future pleasure would have been added a sequence of present desires.

    You wanted to know your future, less to reassure yourself

about what you would become than to live through anticipation the life that awaited you. You used to dream of an exhaustive day planner wherein your days would be recorded up to your death. You would be able to prepare yourself for the joys and trials of the next day as well as those of days far off. You would be able to consult the future like you could remember the past, and circulate there at will. But one day this imaginary planner showed your life to you as a huge, thorny wall. A life foreseen was reassuring to you because you imagined it to be made up of pleasures. In fact nothing stipulated what the day planner would contain. It could have been your worst nightmare, or a sequence of scheduled hardships that you would have no choice but to prepare yourself to brave. Misrecognizing the future, however, could render it desirable.

You used to want only to perform acts that would resonate for a long time, gestures that, though completed in a few minutes, would leave vestiges to persist and continue to be seen. Your interest in painting depended upon this suspension of time in matter: the brief time of its realization is succeeded by the long life of the painting.

During summer, on the coast, you used to sail a catamaran single-handedly. You tightened the ropes and sailed straight ahead. Why tack to the coast when the waves were the same all over? A straight line suited you. You weren't preoccupied with an itinerary; you steered the bow toward the horizon, back turned to the coast. You wanted to forget land, but your expeditions were too brief for you to be surrounded by nothing but sea. Air filled your lungs; waves drowned your hearing; the movement of the boat kept your body occupied as it sought balance. The rocking of the waters hypnotized you at the same time as the wind kept you alert. You liked this lucid somnolence, similar to that of a child rocked by a wet nurse singing the melody in a gentle voice that will put it to sleep. Then you would need to turn back. You would come about and try hard to return as directly as you had left, despite the direction of the wind, which compelled you to tack. The sight of land, far away, brought you back to the reality the sea had made you forget. As you drew nearer to the beach, you would leave behind the waking dream the waves had thrown you into.

One night, in a large town in Provence, you walked for three hours at night through the streets at random. You reached a neighborhood devoid of charm, marked off by two large boulevards. Cheap-looking buildings alternated with housing projects, retirement homes, garages, grocery stores, ladies' hairdressers, and stores selling vacuum cleaners and pet products. A thick odor of frying and of simmering meat escaped from a restaurant cloaked in dirty curtains, where a truck-stop menu was on display. The orange urban lighting ruined the pleasure you would have been able to take in looking at the few villas from a previous century miraculously preserved between two concrete blocks. You came to a small church bordering on a cemetery. The white gravestones, cut off by an entry gate adorned with a large cypress tree, appeared to you as an oasis of calm beauty. You had never before thought to walk in a cemetery alone at night. Guarding against it was your unconscious dread of ghosts. A hook in a stone of the wall and a support high up on the gate made up your mind. Without reflection you started to scale the wall before thinking about how you would get back out. A car came by; you climbed back down to let it pass. Next came a motorcycle, then another car. While waiting you pretended to be looking at the opening and closing hours of the cemetery on a small plaque. It was two in the morning. You started climbing up again, and in a few movements you were inside the outer wall. You didn't know whether the cemetery was guarded like the neighboring building sites. Your steps crunched on the gravel. You were not now afraid of ghosts: you had already been thinking about death so often, for such a long time, that they had become quite familiar to you. To see these graves in the penumbra reassured you, as if you had come to a silent ball organized by benevolent friends. You were the only outsider there, the living person surrounded by recumbent statues that love him. The apparition of a guard or a prowler would have disturbed you more than that of a specter. In this vista of stones softened by darkness, your thoughts floated about as though you were between life and death. You felt a stranger to yourself, but intimately acquainted with this place peopled with the dead. You had rarely experienced this feeling: to be already dead. But, looking at the hills unfolding below the cemetery, where lights were shimmering through the windows of houses, you suddenly returned to the land of the living. A survival instinct then guided your steps toward the exit. Some supports allowed you to scale the wall to get out. While coming down on the road-side of the wall, your foot pushed against the cemetery gate, which opened. It wasn't locked. Access had been freely available: you had climbed over for nothing.

Sun, heat, and light, which delighted those around you, appeared to you as perturbations of your solitude, summons to the outdoors, obligations to joy. You refused to have your euphoria put down to climate. You wanted to be solely responsible for it. If you were asked to do something on account of the good weather, you declined the invitation. Gray weather, winter, rain, or cold did not displease you. Nature then seemed to be in tune with your mood. If the weather was poor, you would be let off the hook, no one would think of reproaching you for not going out. You could stay at your place without the anomalous appearance of your shutting yourself in. No one would come around asking questions about your taste for staying indoors.

You used to say that distinction, which is the opposite of discretion, was too visible a version of elegance. You wanted to be discreet; you were said to be elegant. You would have preferred to be neutral, but your beauty and your stature ensured you were noticed in a crowd. You considered wearing poorly tailored clothing, stooping, making clumsy gestures to efface yourself behind a less desirable façade. But you were afraid that these artifices would themselves be noticed, and would make you seem affected, vain. You therefore resigned yourself to your natural elegance.

In the metro, in Paris, you entered a train car and sat down on a folding seat. Three stations later, a homeless man came to sit next you. He smelled of cheese, urine, and shit. Hirsute, he turned toward you, sniffed several times, and said: "Hmmm, it smells flowery in here." You had put on a fragrance in the morning before going out. For once, a homeless man made you laugh. Normally such people made you uncomfortable. You didn't feel threatened, they'd never caused you any harm, but you were afraid of ending up like them. Nothing justified this fear, however. You were not alone, poor, alcoholic, abandoned. You had a family, a wife, friends, a house. You did not lack money. But homeless people were like ghosts foretelling one of your possible ends. You didn't identify with happy people, and in your excessiveness you projected onto those who had failed in everything, or succeeded in nothing. The homeless embodied the final stage in a decline your life could have tended toward. You did not take them for victims, but for authors of their own lives. As scandalous as it seems, you used to think that some homeless people had chosen to live that way. This was what disturbed you the most: that you could, one day, choose to fall. Not to let yourself go, which would only have been a form of passivity, but to want to descend, to degrade yourself, to become a ruin of yourself. Memories of other homeless people came to your mind. You couldn't prevent yourself, when you saw some, from stopping to watch them at a distance. They owned nothing, lived from day to day without domicile, without possessions, without friends. Their destitution fascinated you. You used to imagine living like them, abandoning what had been given to you and what you had acquired. You would detach yourself from things, from people, and from time. You would situate yourself in a perpetual present. You would renounce organizing your future. You would let yourself be guided by the randomness of encounters and events, indifferent to one choice over another. When, seated in the metro, you were imagining to yourself what it would be like to live in his shoes, your neighbor stood up, staggering, and left to join a group of drunk homeless people on the next metro platform. One of them was slumped on the ground, asleep with his mouth open, belly up, one shoe undone. He resembled a corpse. This was perhaps what you feared: to become inert in a body that still breathes, drinks, and feeds itself. To commit suicide in slow motion.

You had hung up a portrait of your great-uncle in your study, on the wall behind the desk, so that when seated your back was turned to it. You used to say that this way it was him who looked at you, and not the other way round. His eyes were permanently fixed on you, and if you wanted to see him, you had to turn around. As such, when you looked at him, he received your frank, sustained attention, bearing no resemblance to the furtive glances you gave him on entering the room.

In the town where you lived, there were neither psychoanalysts nor psychiatrists. You wondered whether your malaise could be attributed to a physical malfunction. You made an appointment with a general practitioner who prescribed you antidepressants. You took them as an experiment. After a few days, you experienced a feeling of strangeness. You heard words leave your mouth as if they belonged to someone else. Your gestures were brusque. You approached your wife and suddenly took her in your arms. You embraced her violently and then rapidly detached yourself. She watched you brush her aside without understanding why, her arms held out toward you. You next picked up a book and started reading. The words on the page sketched out the lines of an abstract painting; their meaning escaped you. You put it back down; you went into the kitchen and made a sandwich that you didn't eat. You went into the street to take a stroll, and you came back a few minutes later because you didn't know why you had gone out. You smoked a cigarette that you put out after a few drags. You sat down at your work desk and reread the exchange rates before bringing out some bills that needed paying. Nothing kept your attention. You organized files. You thought of the long list of things you had to do without managing to discipline your mind. Agitation led you without logic from one action to another, so that you accomplished none. At night, you were too on edge for sleep. The first few days, you were turned gray by the lack of sleep, as one might be after having stayed up all night. But two weeks later, your sleep reserves had been entirely exhausted. Your insomnia had a mind-numbing effect. You became stupid. Your memory grew weaker. You labored to remember proper names, including those of people you knew well. It took you two days to recall the name of a friend whom you hadn't seen for only a few months. Her face and her voice came to you without difficulty, but her name seemed never to have existed. You only found it by rereading your address book. You went back to the doctor's office, he prescribed you a new antidepressant, which also acted as a sleeping pill. Taking it, you immediately found yourself in a deep sleep, but unfortunately you never really woke from it. During the day you floated in somnolence. You spoke in slow motion, you articulated poorly, you responded to questions only after a delay. Your bearing became heavier. You dragged your heels. Outside, you walked abnormally straight; you avoided obstacles at the last possible moment. Sometimes you disregarded them entirely. You walked through a puddle with indifference; you bumped into a lamppost with your shoulder. Pedestrians turned around to look at you in the street. You lived in an immediate present. Your memory of recent events became thin. You didn't retain the stories just told you. In the middle of an anecdote you were being told, you asked yourself how it had begun. It was only when you repeated some questions, asked again about subjects your interlocutors had just mentioned, that your lacunae were discovered. One week after having started to take the new antidepressant, you had become a ghost. You only emerged from this coma in order to complain about the stupidity it had thrown you into. The doctor, whom you went back to see, prescribed you a third antidepressant. For the first week, no effect could be felt other than loss of sleep. But after the second week, you experienced abnormal excitement at unforeseeable moments. One day you woke up tired. You had slept for only two hours even though you had gone to bed early and had stayed lying down all night. You lived in slow motion until midday, when suddenly, for no reason, euphoria followed. You spoke fast; you busied yourself with random tasks. While on the phone with your mother, you continually modified the position of groceries in the fridge, all the time looking at the rest of the kitchen with a view to the radical changes you suddenly wanted to make to its decoration. Then you brusquely interrupted your conversation to go look for a shovel in the basement. You wanted to clear away a heap of earth in the garden, which had been there for months. The shovel could not be found, but you stumbled onto some moldy old crates that you decided to stack. You took the stack in your arms—it came up to above the top of your head—and walked blindly in the direction of the dump a kilometer away from your house. When you came back you noticed that you had left the doors wide open, and that a casserole was burning on the gas stove. This spectacle disheartened you. You sat down on the couch and felt a violent pain in your temples, as if a caliper were slowly tightening on them. You tapped your fingers on your head; it sounded hollow like a dead man's skull. Suddenly, you no longer had a brain. Or rather, it was another person's brain. You sat like this for two hours, asking yourself if you were yourself. A document sitting next to you on the couch, the edge of which extended into the air, caught your attention. It was the annual report of a big international bank. You didn't know how it had gotten there, but you read it attentively. You didn't really understand what you were reading. It was in French, but nonetheless resembled a foreign language. Having come to the end of this abstract text, which for you possessed the strange charm of poetry in another tongue, you got up and wanted to start a business. You left for the library in order to search through books on the legal statutes governing associations. It was closed, it was Sunday, but you hadn't thought of that. You came back running; your legs were itching; you were overflowing with uncontrollable physical energy. You stopped in front of an old wall, out of which jutted a piece of flint, which you suddenly wanted to eat. It was when you were approaching the rock that you realized how strangely you were behaving. But you just as soon forgot about it. You again took up your uninhibited running. You were hot; it was a fine day; you found the sun exalting. You looked straight at it in defiance, like when you were a child. You had tears in your eyes. The slight pain pleased you. Bedazzlement transformed the street into a white monochrome through which you walked more slowly in order to appreciate its beauty. Colors returned gently, as in a cinematic special effect. This is what gave you the idea to walk in slow motion, to try out another special effect on your body. You took half an hour to reach your house; you crossed the garden like a tortoise. Your wife appeared on the doorstep and began to laugh. You let out an uncontrolled, crazy laugh, which stopped suddenly, and which baffled your wife. You spotted a shutter on which the paint had flaked off, and you undertook to repaint it. The darkness and smell of the junk room where you stored the paintbrushes suddenly brought you back to reality. The familiar smell made you remember your state of mind prior to the antidepressants. You realized how the euphoria they had created was artificial. The down periods that followed this enthusiasm were more intense than before. You had less control over yourself; the medication had taken possession of your moods. Was a little bit of fake happiness worth losing your free will? You decided to give up these chemical crutches, which either split you in two or made you stupid. But your body had become accustomed to them. You needed to make it through two weeks of exhaustion and various new anguishes before becoming yourself again.

If each event consisted of its beginning, its becoming real, and its completion, you would prefer the beginning because there desire wins out over pleasure. In their beginnings, events preserve the potential that they lose in their completion. Desire prolongs itself so long as it is not achieved. As for pleasure, it signals the death of desire, and soon of pleasure itself. It's strange that while loving beginnings, you terminated yourself: suicide is an end. Did you consider it a beginning?

You used to play tennis, squash, and ping-pong. You went horseback riding. You swam. You went running. You went sailing. You would walk through town and countryside. You did not play team sports. You preferred to expend your energy alone, without depending on teammates. You liked playing against an opponent, less in order to beat him than to motivate your own efforts. When you would ride on horseback alone in the countryside, or when you swam in the sea, in rivers, in swimming pools, it sometimes happened that you would, in the middle of your exertions, be discouraged by the absurdity of what you were in the process of doing: athletic exertion was vanity. You engaged in it less for the joy of the act than in order to exhaust yourself. Your body, like that of an animal, produced more energy than necessary. The overabundance of force you accumulated would turn against you if it wasn't depleted. If a week went by without your expending yourself, you would stamp your feet; your muscles would be tense from the moment you woke up and wouldn't relax until nightfall.

In order to measure the effects of depriving yourself in this fashion, you refrained from exercising for a month. No tennis, no horseback riding, no boating, no swimming, no running, no walking. You became electric. Like an overcharged battery, you risked melting or exploding. Your gestures became faster. You felt clumsy manipulating everyday objects, as though you were handling a complex machine for the first time. Long forgotten nervous tics from childhood reappeared. You extended your arms for no reason ten times in a row, making your elbow joints crack. You stretched out your shoulders, forcing the joints to their limits. You breathed in and out exaggeratedly for five minutes. When you were on your feet, you would stand on tip-toes; you contorted your ankles when speaking to a friend who detained you for too long. In your room you felt the urge to box or kick the air. Your body was trying to cheat by expending its energy despite the immobility you were inflicting on it.

One winter morning, you left your house wearing shorts, a T-shirt, and cross-trainers. You took a path along a river that led away from town and snaked through the countryside. It was eight in the morning; dawn was breaking, mist evaporating. The cold pierced your meager clothing; your hands reddened; your ears were freezing. Your body was fragile, as if you were naked in a freezer. You wondered what masochism drove you to inflict this torture on yourself. But you ran fast and your body heated up again. Soon drops of sweat forming beads on your neck and your thighs irritated your skin. You became out of breath; the icy air penetrated into your lungs, which were spitting out the nicotine caked on their walls. But you persevered. After the painful first twenty minutes, you were overcome with euphoria. You forgot the cold then and the pain of the effort. You believed now that you were able to run without limits; your brain had been invaded by a natural drug secreted by your body. You ran for an hour and a half before thinking of turning back. You got home three hours later, drenched, indifferent to the cold and the pain. It was painful, in fact, for you to stop. You breathed hard in the vestibule, skipping on the spot in order to soften the abrupt end of the run. It was too hot in the house. To go out again would have been useless, your body in the process of reacclimatizing itself could not have withstood the outrageous cold. You moved from one room to another. You came across a mirror; your face was covered with red and yellow blotches. You approached the mirror; you recognized your physiognomy, but it seemed to belong to someone else. Fatigue disassociated you from yourself. You looked at the furniture and objects around you. They should have been familiar; they were strangers to you. You picked up a dictionary; you opened it at random and fell on the word *Fraction*, for which you read the definition. Words were abstract paintings. You recognized the letters; you put them together to make harmonious sounds, but no meaning emanated from the sentences you read. The text was opaque like a monochrome surface. You closed the dictionary again and picked up a piece of candy that had left itself on a shelf. You removed its wrapper and put it in your mouth. A strong taste of mint irrigated your palate and spread through your lungs. This pepperminty assault made you cough; you sat down in an armchair; you closed your eyes and lolled backwards to rest your head. Blood beat strong through your heart. Heavier than usual. Your veins and your arteries seemed too narrow. Your flesh was loud. It didn't produce music, but a sickening pulsation, and you waited for the abatement of this rhythm. Your neck was sawed at by the wooden backrest it was resting on. You got up. Changing position made you dizzy. White spots gathered on the surface of your eyes. They masked the décor; the furniture disappeared. Just as you were about to faint, a chill ran down your spine. The white spots blurred, objects faded back in, like in a slideshow, but they felt no more real than the spots. You dropped onto the sofa; its velvet caressed you, but no memories accompanied this sensation. Your memory seemed to have been eradicated. You moved toward a photograph of your wife on a bookshelf. You looked at it with indifference, as if it were a portrait of a stranger put up in a photo booth. While you were worrying about your lack of feeling, you heard steps on the parquet. You turned around; it was your wife who was telling you about a dinner to which you had both been invited the following week, and which she supposed you would refuse to attend. A refusal fell out of your mouth before you had thought about what you wanted to say. Your wife showed astonishment at your abruptness, but all you could see was an abstract grimace. It really was her, you recognized her, but you wondered if you knew her. She was abstract like the other objects in the depths from which her silhouette emerged. She was looking at you, she was expecting a reaction from you, but your face remained inexpressive. The physical excess of the run had plunged you into a waking sleep from which you couldn't wake. Whatever was happening between your temples and between your eyes and the back of your skull no longer belonged to you. You were guided by automatic physical reactions. You then headed toward the bathroom to take a shower. The cold of the tiles under your feet, the smell of soap, the hot water that streamed onto your skull didn't succeed in bringing you out of your torpor. You lay down after the shower, but sleep didn't come. You were separated from yourself, so relaxed as to be without sensation. Your indifference should have made you afraid, but you were indifferent to indifference. You got up, you dressed, and you rejoined your wife for lunch. At the table, you reacted to her conversation with vague, pat phrases that implied no response. You passed the day like a sleepwalker, till nightfall. When you turned on the lights, seven hours had passed since your run. You started to wake up. Your physical expenditure had exhausted you. You decided, in the future, to economize your efforts so that they wouldn't backfire. You would have to feel out the right amount of exercise, so that it would relax you without annihilating you.

Your end was premeditated. You had conceived of a scenario where your body would be found immediately after your death. You didn't want it to stay there decomposing for days, for it to be found rotten like that of some forgotten hermit. You did violence to your living body, but you didn't want it to be found, in death, victim to degradations other than those you had inflicted on it yourself. You made sure to appear to your wife, and to those who would carry your body away, in the way you had planned.

You spoke little, but with precision, and with passion when speaking to someone you knew. You weren't urbane. At a party, you wouldn't head toward strangers to start up a conversation. You became acquainted with new people if they spoke to you. Though you knew how to speak with whomever you wanted, you preferred asking questions to making assertions. You could listen endlessly to someone answering your questions, or to several people speaking together on a subject that you had brought up. Not liking to speak about yourself in public, your questions allowed you to hide yourself behind the position of listener.

At night you perceived the flow of time less. Urbane duties were again put off until the next day. No social act needed to be undertaken; there was nothing to distract you from yourself any longer. You became contemplative without guilt, and without any limits beyond your fatigue.

Over the course of your sleepless nights, eyes closed, time did away with itself, thoughts and scenarios looped through your brain with the regularity of a clock. Like an adult looking at a merry-go-round designed for children, you observed the spinning of your reveries. They brought buried memories back to your consciousness, which disappeared the moment you recognized them and reappeared at the next turn before disappearing anew.

You watched scenes unfurl, a passive spectator, as though at a film. By dint of being repeated, the actions you saw lost their meaning. You couldn't have said how long each scene lasted, nor how long you spent watching them. You wouldn't turn on the light in order to check the time, but when day broke through the shutters, you believed you hadn't slept a moment since going to bed. Your wife affirmed to you, however, on waking, that she had heard you murmur incomprehensible phrases in your sleep. You had slept without perceiving it. You confused sleep with wakefulness.

You told me two of your dreams. In the first, you hold in your hand a pink card on which is written in red italics, *The Eternal Roe-Deer*. You understand the coded message; it is a wedding invitation from an old friend with whom you have been out of touch for the past ten years. The wedding takes place that very day in Finland. A helicopter sets you down above a fjord. Below, tables are set and assembled people greet you from afar as an important guest. You hear all their conversations distinctly and simultaneously, even though they are taking place three hundred meters down below. You look again at the invitation card, which is enough to transport you to the middle of the party, where all the women are your former lovers. At five o'clock, the parents of the newlyweds undress and dive into the fjord. The guests follow suit. The water has a taste of sweetened gooseberry and is breathable. In this ideal amniotic liquid, you make love with your former lovers, one after the other. They love each other as much as you love them.

In the second dream, you try to escape an armed man who is following you through an opera house over the course of a performance of *Norma*. You fight violently, starting up again several times, but neither of you gets the upper hand, except at the end of the performance, when your adversary manages to force you into a small room that hangs over the auditorium, and where "a very unusual man, who will be happy to meet you" is waiting for you. In this room there are computers and video screens. The man is mostly turned away from you, you don't see his face. It's not until you come closer, circling around him, that you discover, terrified, that it's not a man, but an android robot of yellow chromed metal. It looks at you with cold eyes, shows you to your seat, and starts a video where you are seen on an operating table, confident, yawning as you fall asleep under the effects of the anesthetic. Surgical implements—in fact, instruments of torture—come down from box beams concealed in the ceiling. An articulated arm that has several needles on it reaches out toward your testicles, which a mechanical hand has just ligatured. You realize that, in the recent past, you've been kidnapped and operated upon without your knowledge.

You preferred the first dream, but the pleasure you felt having the one and the unease with which you dived into the other did nothing to alter the charm of recalling them. Dream or nightmare, what did it matter, if you could experience the confusion of reliving, while awake, the memory of things lived in sleep.

You left one day to walk along a beach in Normandy at low tide with your brother and sister. You were barefoot, in a bathing suit. The immense stretch of sand and water resembled a desert. It was during the week, in the off-season. There was nothing to do other than to walk, to look at the sea in the distance and the houses along the coast. While you remained silent and contemplative, your thoughts tossed here and there by the rhythm of your steps, your brother and your sister talked among themselves. They told each other funny stories, invented simple games, ran laughing, jumped in pools where they tried to catch shrimp and little fish with their hands. You didn't join in their games. You thought of things unrelated to the setting in which you found yourself. This landscape was not, for you, a place to live, but a backdrop in which to float. You looked at your brother and sister; their bodies were alike, but you resembled neither. They were so happy together that they didn't wonder why you were distant. You were their older brother, you had seen them be born and grow up. To be reminded of the differences that separated you gave you the impression of being a stranger to your family.

One July, when you were seventeen years old, you had dinner with some friends of your mother in the garden in front of the house. The table was set in front of the big open doors of the living room, on the old slabs of stone that marked the threshold of the vegetable garden. Among the six guests was a psychoanalyst, about fifty years old. You took it upon yourself to bring out the dishes that your mother had prepared. The kitchen was far away, you had to cross the old kitchen, the entrance, go along a hallway, and then pass through a small living room as well as the main living room in order finally to arrive at the table set in the place that you had chosen. You rarely dined there, your mother preferred the convenience of the dining room, and she was afraid of the cold when night fell. But you liked the view of the vegetable garden. The central path divided into three after about fifteen meters, and the side paths gave the garden the air of a nursery labyrinth. You had set down some candles on the table, in anticipation of evening. When it came, you lit them and they spread a soft light over the faces of the guests. The conversation was relaxed, you tasted the simple happiness of an agreeable meal in the company of intelligent adults. You participated in their exchanges, you were encouraged in your reasoning, which was thought to be quite daring for someone of your age. The psychoanalyst applied the following phrase to someone of whom you had spoken, who would endlessly apologize to justify the mistakes he made: "A self excused is a self accused." When the time for dessert came, you went to the kitchen to look for the strawberry charlotte you had spent several hours making. You served the guests one by one, ending with yourself. You reflected on what the psychoanalyst had said and delayed tasting the dessert. The guests ate it slowly, in small spoonfuls, without saying anything. No one complimented you, as you would have expected them to do. You understood why after your first spoonful. The charlotte was salty. You then said: "But how could I have been such an idiot as to confuse sugar with salt?" The psychoanalyst retorted: "A self accused is a self excused."

You dreaded the boredom of being alone, as well as the boredom of being with several people. But most of all you dreaded two-person boredom, the face-to-face. You attributed no virtue whatsoever to moments of waiting, moments without anything perceptible at stake. You believed that only action and thought, which seemed absent here, carry life. You underestimated the value of passivity, which is not the art of pleasing but of placing oneself. Being in the right place at the right time requires accepting long moments of boredom, passed in gray spaces. Your impatience deprived you of the art of succeeding by being bored.

It was eight in the evening when you arrived with your wife at Christophe's garden for a barbeque with friends you knew during high school. You hadn't kept up contact with anyone from that era except for him. You no longer socialized with any of the people reunited this evening, but, thinking back on them the night before, you were excited by the memories that came back to you. You thought that seeing them again would reunite past years and the future prospect of seeing them, in the present.

There were, in this big bourgeois house in the middle of town, a dozen couples. The girls and boys of your adolescence had come with their companions. They were now adults; some of them were accompanied by their children. You looked at their faces and appreciated the strange impression of seeing the memories you had of them superimposed upon their current faces, as in films, one body transforming into another in a few seconds. But, as you watched, today's faces didn't manage to efface the old ones imprinted in your memory. You would no doubt have needed to see these people for some time in order for the present to replace the past, and for your mental identity files to fix upon the morphologies now in front of you. This evening, if you were speaking to a woman, and you turned away for a few minutes, when you looked at her a second time the two images became confused all over again. You spent part of the evening playing with these disturbances of perception, like dressing a doll with only two outfits at your disposal. But if you wanted to, you could also dismiss the old images and speak to these people as if they were new acquaintances. Whereas, on the contrary, if you concentrated on the past, the words that they pronounced would reach you as a distant murmur, a speech given by a character from a dream, in a foreign language, yet made up of familiar sounds.

Christophe had prepared beef and pork, sausages and potatoes, which he had cooked on the two barbecues set up a few meters away from the tables covered in paper tablecloths. Plates, cutlery, and plastic cups were put at the guests' disposal. Several boxes of cheap wine, white and red, awaited drinkers next to the fruit juice and cheap sodas. Usually, this kind of crude menu would bother you, all the more so in that the smoke set off in its preparation would smother the gathering if the wind blew in the wrong direction, and would leave its odor on their clothing until the next day. But this evening, nothing disturbed you. Though the charm of the beautiful garden, adorned with lilacs in flower, was wasted on you. The rediscovery of these old acquaintances gave you so much pleasure that the scene could have unfurled anywhere. Your wife beamed with the joy of seeing you happy; she who, not knowing anyone, could not partake in the euphoria of the grand reunion. She felt herself to be an outsider to the scene, yet familiar with all the people, since they were familiar to you. You paid no attention to your happiness, up until the moment when you understood, looking at her, just how happy you were to be there. She was your mirror.

Christophe came over with a plate he had prepared for you.

Touched by his attention, you took it and began eating. The dishes were overcooked; part of the meat had been turned into charcoal. But these details did not diminish your joy, perhaps they even constituted it, since you could not attribute your happiness to anything other than the people reunited here, even their imperfections.

While night fell and the hours passed, you spoke now to some, now to others. When you were addressing an old friend, in a tête-à-tête, you came to believe your words were the right ones. But when speaking to two people at once, you tried to find words that could touch both of them at the same time. You rarely succeeded: the proximity of bodies, which demonstrated their singularity, reminded you how difficult it is to speak simultaneously to two. If, however, as happened later, you told a story to a group gathered together to listen to you, your words no longer sought to address themselves to anyone in particular, and what you said could be received by everyone in his own manner, without you concerning yourself with who had understood what. You no longer saw anyone in particular, only a group where individualities dissolved. You needed, in order to speak comfortably, to be as close as possible to your listeners when in dialogue, or as far as possible from them when making a speech. In between, you felt misunderstood.

Toward three in the morning, while you were holding your wife's hand, listening to Christophe make all the guests laugh, none of whom had left yet, you thought back to the conversations you had been having. You'd passed from one old friend to another, you had told stories to groups of a few people at a time, and you had succeeded finally in speaking to couples without being at a loss for words. This party, to which you had come without conviction, ended up enchanting you. You belonged to a community united by memories. Later, none of the guests at the party believed, when they heard what happened, that you were already thinking of suicide then.

You knew that some of those close to you would feel guilty at not having anticipated your choice to die, and that they would deplore their inability to help you to want to live. But you thought them mistaken. No one other than yourself could have given you a greater taste for life than for death. You imagined scenes in which someone tried to cheer you up, as a mother might take her melancholy child by the hand and show it things she believes will make it happy. The repulsion that then took hold of you did not come from your rejection of this well-meaning woman, nor from the nature of the supposed objects of joy that she would show you, but from the fact that the desire to live could not be dictated to you. You could not be happy on command, whether the order was given by you or by someone else. The moments of happiness you knew came unbidden. You could understand their sources, but you could not reproduce them.

In a vintage store, you bought a pair of discreetly elegant black leather English shoes. The high-quality leather was almost new, yet it bore the imprint of its previous owner. The fronts of the shoes were creased according to the shape of his feet, which were similar to your own. When you tried them on in the store, they adapted themselves perfectly to your morphology, as if you had been wearing them for months. You were in the habit of hesitating when buying clothing. Your wardrobe was already well stocked, and since it only contained plain and simple clothing, it would never go out of fashion. To buy new clothing would only have been necessary if the old were worn out. It wasn't money that guided your choices, but your mania for collecting nearly identical outfits. You used to choose, in stores, an improved version of what you already owned, in order to constitute the perfect assortment, the universal uniform freeing you of the daily duty of choosing how to dress yourself. Even though you knew that this uniform did not exist, you continued on your quest. Despite the numerous pairs of black leather shoes you already possessed, you decided to acquire this new pair. Finding them by chance in a vintage store appeared to you to be a sign. You did not yet know of what. Though you would find out soon enough. A few days later, you went to an informational meeting held by a green party campaigning in the general elections. You went alone, and, after the speeches, you were hanging around the buffet, inclined to converse with the militants. The environmentalists attracted you for their ideas, but you didn't believe them capable of governing wisely once elected. A couple came up to you. The man spoke of the importance of preserving regional cultures, particularly languages, in the face of globalization, and the increasingly widespread use of English. You listened to his conventional remarks while responding with nods of the head, which let him believe that you agreed. His wife, by his side, remained silent. Until her face suddenly collapsed. She fixed her eyes on you, dropped them, and fixed them on you anew. These backs and forths made her nervous. She left to get herself a glass of white wine. Her behavior disturbed you and plunged you deeper into silence. The man kept on speaking to you until, faced with your lack of reaction, he took his leave of you and made off toward someone else. You went back to the buffet to ask the waiter for another drink, and once you were served, as you cleared a trail through the militants, you stumbled across the wife. She asked you to follow her so she could talk to you away from the crowd. She was on the verge of tears; her lips were trembling. She had recognized the shoes you were wearing. They were the ones that she had given to her nephew, and which his mother had sold after he committed suicide.

You did not have children. Your wife had asked you if you wanted any. You didn't feel ready yet, and you didn't know if you ever would be. To procreate was such an important and such a mysterious act that you did not believe yourself capable of doing it wisely. You had to accept not being able to measure up to your capacity to transmit life. You did not think that, when they conceived you, your parents were any more reasonable than you currently were. Guessing at the selfishness and the levity of their decision distressed you. So you came to believe that you had been less desired for what you were than for what they imagined you would be. You felt like an impostor, because you knew that, though you had not disappointed them, you never resembled the dreams they had built around you. However, you did not know anything about these dreams, since you had never asked your parents to tell you about them. Why have a child? In order to prolong life, and for the sake of curiosity about what your offspring might look like. You reached a point of thinking that the life you were leading was not worth prolonging. But your child would not be you. It would be itself. There was no reason to believe that you would pass your sadness on to it. Might it not be, on the contrary, destined for happiness? Yet, rather than giving your wife an answer, you remained evasive. Awaiting an enthusiasm you did not show, she took your silence for a refusal. You died without descendents.

As my thoughts turn to you again, I do not suffer. I do not miss you. You are more present in my memory than you were in the life we shared. If you were still alive, you would perhaps have become a stranger to me. Dead, you are as alive as you are vivid.

Your desire to die was less strong at night than during the day and less strong in the morning than in the afternoon.

You did not leave a letter to those close to you, explaining your death. Did you know why you wanted to die? If you did, why not write it down? Out of fatigue from living and disdain for leaving traces that would survive you? Or because the reasons that were pushing you to disappear seemed empty? Maybe you wanted to preserve the mystery of your death, thinking that nothing should be explained. Are there good reasons for committing suicide?

Those who survived you asked themselves these questions; they will not find answers.

Your mother cried for you when she learned of your death. She cried for you every day until your burial. She cried for you alone, in her husband's arms, in the arms of your brother and your sister, in the arms of her mother and your wife. She cried for you during the ceremony, following your coffin to the cemetery, and during your inhumation. When friends, many of them, came to present their condolences, she cried for you. With every hand that she shook, with every kiss she received, she again saw fragments of your past, of the days she believed you to be happy. Faced with your death, scenarios of what you could have lived or experienced with these people, gave them a feeling of immense loss: you had, by your suicide, saddened your past and abolished your future. Your mother cried for you in the days following your funeral, and she cried for you again, alone, whenever she thought of you. Years later, there are many, like her, whose tears flow whenever they think of you.

Regrets? You had some for causing the sadness of those who cried for you, for the love they felt for you, and which you had returned. You had some for the solitude in which you left your wife, and for the emptiness your loved ones would experience. But these regrets you felt merely in anticipation. They would disappear along with you: your survivors would be alone in carrying the pain of your death. This selfishness of your suicide displeased you. But, all things considered, the lull of death won out over life's painful commotion.

You wrote a collection of verses, brief and condensed, like your life. You told nobody about them. Your wife discovered them after your death in your desk drawer:

        Ferns caress me
        Nettles sting me
        Brambles scratch me

        The city hones me
        The house welcomes me
        The bedroom calms me

        The enemy encourages me
        Combat excites me
        Victory leaves me indifferent

        Day dazzles me
        Evening soothes me
        Night envelops me

Dominating oppresses me
Subjugating enslaves me
Being alone frees me

Heat bothers me
Rain closes me in
Cold awakens me

Tobacco irritates me
Alcohol tranquilizes me
Drugs isolate me

Evil surprises me
Forgetting is desirable to me
Laughter saves me

Wishing carries me
Pleasure disappoints me
Desire picks me up again

Friendship ties me
Love reveals me
Sex delights me

Accumulation tempts me
Keeping reassures me
Daring relieves me

The sun wearies me
The earth surrounds me
The moon moves me

SUICIDE

Life is proposed to me
My name is passed on to me
My body is imposed on me

Television depresses me
Radio disturbs me
Newspapers bore me

Saints fascinate me
The faithful intrigue me
Priests disquiet me

What is unique surprises me
What is double resembles me
What is triple reassures me

Equilibrium maintains me
Falling reveals me
Recovery exhausts me

A single point hypnotizes me
A constellation scatters me
A line guides me

Time is lacking for me
Space is enough for me
The void attracts me

The basement repels me
The attic appeals to me
The staircase guides me

Talent charms me
Virtuosity fools me
Genius illuminates me

Prudence agitates me
Violence excites me
Vengeance disappoints me

Thirst bothers me
Hunger enlivens me
Eating puts me to sleep

The edge tempts me
The hole draws me
The bottom alarms me

The truth moves me
Uncertainty bothers me
Falsehood fascinates me

Gossip misleads me
Polemic enflames me
Silence redeems me

Obstacles raise me
Defeat hardens me
Success mollifies me

Error instructs me
Habit improves me
Perfection obsesses me

SUICIDE

Offenses surprise me
Retorts come slowly from me
Contempt avenges me

Perdition tempts me
Irony neutralizes me
Affection redeems me

Faith rattles me
Fidelity suits me
Treason stabs me

Departures delight me
Voyages numb me
Arrivals revive me

Earth bears me
Sand slows me
Mud traps me

Euphoria dissuades me
Innuendo disquiets me
Neutrality convinces me

Sermons annoy me
Examples persuade me
Action vindicates me

Cleaning bores me
Tidying calms me
Discarding delivers me

The new attracts me
The old anchors me
Change animates me

Work fulfills me
Hobbies instruct me
Holidays sedate me

To know makes me grow
Not to know harms me
To forget frees me

Losing is bothersome to me
Winning is a matter of indifference to me
To play is disappointing to me

To deny tempts me
To affirm excites me
To suggest is enough for me

Seducing seduces me
Loving transforms me
Separating pains me

Clothing announces me
Disguises hide me
Uniforms efface me

Speaking commits me
Listening teaches me
Silence tempers me

Birth befalls me
Life occupies me
Death completes me

To climb is difficult for me
To descend is easy for me
To be stationary is useless to me

Homage obliges me
Oration touches me
Eulogy buries me

The flash blinds me
The beam dazzles me
The reflection intrigues me

Speaking identifies me
Shouting frees me
Whispering imposes on me

Humming rocks me
Intoning suspends me
Singing unfolds me

The beginning enthuses me
The middle sustains me
The end disappoints me

Goodness impresses me
Stupidity amuses me
Malice disgusts me

November upsets me
April refreshes me
September soothes me

Envy indisposes me
Jealousy moves me to pity
Hatred distances me

Yesterday wearies me
Sleep immobilizes me
Awakening attacks me

The millennium enfolds me
The century situates me
The decade decorates me

The hour rules me
The minute hurries me
Seconds escape me

Threats fool me
Anguish moves me
Fear excites me

Surprise displeases me
Improvisation harms me
Announcements buttress me

Traps seduce me
Liars fool me
Informers horrify me

SUICIDE

The baroque sickens me
The gothic chills me
Novels enlighten me

Red irritates me
Black moves me
White calms me

The solo attracts me
The quartet sustains me
The symphony distances me

Rules serve me
Constraints stimulate me
Obligation extinguishes me

Dialogue binds me
Monologue imposes upon me
Soliloquy isolates me

The air penetrates me
The ground resists me
The underground smothers me

Rhythm leads me
Melody charms me
Harmony troubles me

Aquariums sadden me
Aviaries oppress me
Cages revolt me

Rain doubles me up
Snow enchants me
Hail stops me

My finger draws
My hand catches
My arm enlaces

My brain conceives
My eye guides
My body makes

The first time tempts me
Its sequel accustoms me
The last depresses me

Tiredness calms me
Lassitude discourages me
Exhaustion stops me

Constructing obsesses me
Conserving calms me
Destroying relieves me

Arriving changes me
Staying costs me
Leaving animates me

The group oppresses me
Solitude holds me
Madness stalks me

SUICIDE

To please pleases me
To displease displeases me
To be indifferent is indifferent to me

Age overtakes me
Youth abandons me
Memory remains with me

Happiness precedes me
Sadness follows me
Death awaits me

AFTERWORD

Edouard Levé committed suicide on October 15, 2007. Ten days earlier he had given a manuscript to his editor; it was a novel entitled *Suicide*, the same you hold in your hands.

Suicide's reception in France has been deeply influenced by the circumstances of the author's death. Although it is a fictional work, written in the second person about a friend of the narrator's who had committed suicide twenty years earlier, its title and subject matter ensure that, despite reports that Levé did leave a suicide note, the present text is taken as a sort of literary explanation of his decision to die. Levé's readers are left to ask, along with the narrator of *Suicide*:

> Did you know why you wanted to die? If you did, why not write it down? Out of fatigue from living and disdain for leaving traces that would survive you? Or because the reasons that were pushing you to disappear seemed empty? Maybe you wanted to preserve the mystery of your death, thinking that nothing should be explained. Are there good reasons for committing suicide? Those who survived you

asked themselves these questions; they will not find answers.

Suicide demands interpretation. No one who reads this novel and knows of Levé's suicide (and its timing guarantees that nearly every reader does know of it) can avoid projecting Levé's questions back onto his own choice of death.

To what extent can we conflate Levé's characters and their motivations with the author and his? The "you" of the novel shares at least two factual details with Levé's life: each were born in winter, and each ended his life by his own hand. But we can find Levé in the artistic method and philosophy of *Suicide*'s "I" as much as we can in the taste for sparseness and stoicism of *Suicide*'s "you." The narrator claims that

> [t]o portray your life in order would be absurd: I remember you at random. My brain resurrects you through stochastic details, like picking marbles out of a bag.

This stochastic, yet formally constrained, method of "picking marbles out of a bag" is present in all of Levé's writing. In this regard Levé owes a self-acknowledged debt to the writers of the Oulipo group, especially Georges Perec. The opening sentence of Levé's *Autoportrait*—a novel without paragraph breaks consisting of facts about the author as well as his opinions—reads:

> Adolescent je croyais que *La Vie mode d'emploi* m'aiderait à vivre, et *Suicide mode d'emploi* à mourir.[1]
>
> As an adolescent I believed that [Perec's] *Life A User's*

---

1. Levé, Edouard. *Autoportrait*. Paris: P.O.L, 2008, p. 7.

Manual would help me to live, and that [Claude Guillon and Yves le Bonniec's] *Suicide A User's Manual* would help me to die.

Stylistic and thematic elements of *Suicide* were already present in Levé's *Autoportrait*. This is not unusual for Levé's works, which frequently announce or contain later works in embryonic form. For example, *Œuvres* (2002) consists of the author's description of 533 imagined *œuvres* (works). Levé brought some of these works to completion later. In 2006, for example, he published *Amérique*, consisting of images of arbitrary parts of obscure American towns named after grander world cities—Florence, Berlin, Jericho, Oxford, Stockholm, Rio, Delhi, Amsterdam, Paris, Rome, Mexico, Lima, Versailles, Calcutta and Baghdad.[2]

Levé was born in 1965 and died in 2007 at the age of forty-two. He completed his university studies at a prestigious business school, the ESSEC in Paris. In 1991 he began painting. After a life-changing two-month trip to India in 1995, he renounced painting in favor of conceptual photography and writing. Levé referred to himself, flippantly but nonetheless tellingly, as a literary cubist. However, where the historical cubists were vibrant, Levé is austere; his works do not, as do the works of Braque or Picasso, explode the object to reveal its essence better than could a single perspective.

His photographs come in sets, each image arranged around a subject that acts as a center of gravity for the series as a whole. For example, the set called *Rugby* consists of a series of photos of men in business attire ostensibly playing the titular sport.

---

2. In 2009, two years after Levé's suicide, the writer Gérard Gavarry published *Expérience d'Edward Lee, Versailles*, a series of fragmentary texts, each using one of the photos in *Amérique* as a starting point. "Edward Lee" is Gavarry's Americanization of "Edouard Levé."

The arrangement of figures in each shot is as banal as possible, recalling clichéd rugby photographs in a Sunday newspaper: a scrum-half passing a ball to his backline from behind the scrum; a lineout at the moment of the throw-in; a team celebrating after a try. In *Pornography*, shot in a studio with monochrome white background and stark lighting, people are portrayed in a range of sexual positions requiring various degrees of gymnastic ability. The figures are fully dressed. Their faces, again, are impassive. In a series called *Homonyms*, Levé takes neutral frontal portraits of "ordinary" people who happen to share a name with someone famous. The faces of Yves Klein or André Breton, for example, are on display. But of course not *the* Yves Klein, or *the* André Breton. This gesture is repeated when the "you" of *Suicide*, walking through Bordeaux, sees on a brass plaque the words "Charles Dreyfus, Psychoanalyst." *Angoisse* (Anguish), is a collection of shots of a peculiarly tranquil small French town by that name. Particularly memorable examples include photos of a sign proclaiming "Bienvenue à l'Angoisse" (Welcome to Anguish).

In each case, the photos cumulatively cement our feeling that names are not transparent. We do not think of this particular Yves Klein when the name "Yves Klein" pops up; the name "Paris" does not evoke the town we see in the photo; "Angoisse" is not a description of what we feel when looking at that town. These sets of images are not simply about something in the world—rugby, sex—but about (photographic) representations of these things—rugby photography, pornography. Levé ensures that we cannot see such images and naively believe in the objective realism to which photography all too easily lays claim: we no longer take such photos to show the truth about sex and rugby, we automatically see the conventions governing such images.

Levé's writing and his photography reveal a single aesthetic, not dissimilar to that employed by both *Suicide*'s narrator and its "you." *Journal* (2004) takes the form of a newspaper: it is divided into sections, like "Internationale," "Société," "Sports," "Culture," and "Météo" (weather). Each of these sections contains articles, much like the ones to be found in any newspaper, except that they lack proper names: cities, countries, presidents, diseases, writers, and sports stars all appear anonymously. Like his photography, Levé's writing here is stark and austere. He uses a doubly constrained form, choosing to adhere closely to the format of newspaper articles and choosing to eschew proper names, but nonetheless producing a diverse range of content.

There is a tension in Levé's work between the unfinished, incomplete, or possible, and the finished, complete, or fixed. What is the difference between *Amérique* and the other, uncompleted, works described in *Œuvres*? *Suicide* seems to suggest that neither *Amérique*, in its full material embodiment, nor the 532 other *œuvres*, still in their embryonic conceptual form, were truly fixed before October 15, 2007. Levé's death retroactively changed the significance of all of his works. As Sartre famously argued, an oeuvre, with the death of its author, gains a certain coherence. Levé writes:

> Only the living seem incoherent. Death closes the series of events that constitutes their lives. So we resign ourselves to finding a meaning for them. To refuse them this would amount to accepting that a life, and thus life itself, is absurd. Yours had not yet attained the coherence of things done. Your death gave it this coherence.

Levé's death lends to his works the significance of augury. He writes:

> The way in which you quit it rewrote the story of your life in a negative form. Those who knew you reread each of your acts in the light of your last.

> Henceforth, the shadow of this tall black tree hides the forest that was your life. When you are spoken of, it begins with recounting your death, before going back to explain it. Isn't it peculiar how this final gesture inverts your biography?

And the effect of this "inverted biography" on us, his audience, is dramatic:

> Your suicide has become the foundational act . . . Your final second changed your life in the eyes of others. You are like the actor who, at the end of the play, with a final word, reveals that he is a different character than the one he appeared to be playing.

The narrator of *Suicide* attributes to his "you" a strong desire for redemption in a single act, for a retroactive recasting of all his previous deeds in light of his final decision, for a reversal whereby the last would come first. Fittingly, his last work is his first work to appear in English.

Translating this work, I have benefited greatly from the institutional support provided by the American University of Paris, and particularly from its Master's program in Cultural Translation. I am grateful to Anne-Marie Picard-Drillien and Lisa Damon for their help with difficult or colloquial passages in the French, and to Caitlin Dolan-Leach and Harriet Lye for their remarks on and suggestions for the English. I am indebted above all to my mentor Dan Gunn, who has generously pored over this translation with me from beginning to end, and from whom I never cease learning.

JAN STEYN, MARCH 2010

Edouard Levé was born on January 1, 1965 in Neuilly-sur-Seine. A writer, photographer, and visual artist, Levé was the author of four books of prose—*Œuvres*, *Journal*, *Autoportrait*, and *Suicide*—and three books of photographs. *Suicide*, published in 2008, was his final book.

Jan Steyn is Associate Professor and the Director of the MFA in Literary Translation at the University of Iowa.

www.ingramcontent.com/pod-product-compliance
Lightning Source LLC
Jackson TN
JSHW020328160625
86038JS00001B/1